ourn *mörn, mörn,* (*rāre*) be
sorrowful: to wear mour
v.t. to grieve for: to utte —*n.*
mourn'er one who mourn al,
especially a relative of the to
lament or weep for the al
meeting (*U.S.*).—*adj.* **mourn ful** causing, suggesting,
or expressing sorrow: feeling grief.—*adv.* **mourn'fully.**
—*n.* ead: 'fulness.—*adj.* **mourn'ing** grieving:
lamen **ourn'ful** the act of expressing grief: the dress of
mourn **ing grie** ther tokens of mourning—also (*Scot.*) in
pl —*adv.* **ourn'ingly.**—**mourn'ing-band'** a band of
of exterial worn round the sleeve or (*hist.*) the hat.
kens of y that one is in mourning: **mourn'ing-bord'er** a
y.—mo rgin used on notepaper, etc., by those in mour-
ound th dirty edge on a finger-nail (*coll.*): **mourn'ing=**
in mourn e sweet scabious (*Scabiosa atropurpurea*):
notepap **ng-cloak'** an undertaker's cloak, formerly worn
a fi eral: **mourn'ing-coach'** a closed carriage for
abiou mourners to a funeral: **mourn'ing-dove'** an
underta can pigeon with plaintive note: **mourn'ing-piece**
ing-c ure intended to be a memorial of the dead:
a fu n'ing-ring' a ring worn in memory of a dead
plai n: **mourn'ing-stuff** a lustreless black dress fabric,
be pe, cashmere, etc., for making mourning clothes.
wo
f a l
., f
alf;
token

MOURNING HAS

BROKEN

Donald McGurgan

Mourning Has Broken

Donald McGurgan

The Author

Donald (Don) McGurgan lives in Omagh, County Tyrone in Northern Ireland. He has worked in the Electricity Industry as a Wayleave Officer for over 40 years. He is also a successful sound engineer and local historian. He, together with his son Johnny own and run Sounds Good Entertainment. During the lockdown, along with Declan Forde he hosted, produced and broadcast the popular 'Sweet Omagh Town Internet Radio' podcast series on YouTube which details the history of the area with interviews from the past and the present. He has worked for Radio Ulster & Radio Foyle in his career but ultimately his passion has been to help people.

He was a volunteer counsellor with Cruse Bereavement Support for over 10 years where he aided numerous clients with the aid of his own experiences in their personal grief journeys. It is these experiences which drove him to write this book in order to help others who feel that they don't have anyone to talk to in their time of need. He now counsels privately. If you want to contact Donald you can email him on: mcgurgan155@btinternet.com

Disclaimer

ISBN: 978-1-0369-0127-1

'About a week before Marian McGurgan passed way, I rang Don. During the course of our conversation, I heard her asking him, 'Is that Frank?' When Don said it was, she said, 'Hi Frank!' I said 'Hello Marian' and that was the last time I heard her warm and gentle voice.

I'm glad I said hello, simply that...as goodbye would not have done justice to a beloved wife and mother who has remained with Donald, Maria and Jonathan ever since. When I saw Don's title 'Mourning Has Broken' I was reminded of the morning when his heart and those of his children were broken, and my poem 'Just Perfect' was born out of that memory.

We've had many chats over the years about grief - my brother Tom died at ten years old, and was the catalyst for my first putting pen to paper. This book will stir up many memories for those whose grief is raw or indeed a footnote in the past which has never been dealt with. Crucially, I hope - as I have - that you will derive both consolation and hope from the following pages.

Thank you Donald, and very importantly, thank you Marian.'

Just Perfect...
(In memory of Marian McGurgan) November 2000

> *That morning, your family had left Woodbank Road,*
> *And I landed from Derry to find you alone.*
> *We sat beside the coffin but not in the way*
> *That awkward men do...no, it was 'Just perfect'.*

> *'Just perfect, Frank,' you said, 'Just perfect'*
> *Marian's last words before an imperfect world*
> *Took her from you...but her farewell gave you*
> *Strength...her strength, forged in pain...and love.*

1

As I drove back, between the Strule and Foyle,
I imagined you, still alone, but not on your own,
Marian smiling in the Arvalee clouds,
'Just Perfect, Donald'...she reaches out.

Frank Galligan
TV Presenter with Irish TV,
Radio Presenter & Journalist.

'To live in hearts we leave behind is not to die.'

Those lines from Thomas Campbell's poem 'Hallowed Ground' (1825) have provided a balm and comfort, for many years, for those coping and coming to terms with loss. However, for some people grief can be overwhelming and unbearable. We are not taught how to grieve and mourn and each one of us has to find our own way through that ultimate emotional labyrinth.

In this book Donald McGurgan eschews a definitive pathway to the grieving process. Rather, he reflects upon his own life experiences and his many years as a bereavement counsellor. The book raises more questions than answers and therein lies it's strength. This author knows that we are all unique individuals who have to face loss in our own way and his book has the tone of a supportive, listening counsellor.

Mourning Has Broken is a welcome companion on a hard road.

Declan Forde
Artist, Writer, Poet, Teacher & Singer

'Bereavement to me at times is like searching in the fog for something you know you will never find. My personal thought about death is like the preparation for a New Dawn. Bereavement allows you to thank God for all those memories that you make. It is the price you pay for loving someone.

Bereavement enables you to put that 'special love' safely in your heart where it will remain safe for ever.'

Roley McIntyre
Cruise Beravement Counsellor
& New Dawn Counselling

'Grief happens in instalments. Just when we think we are over it, and we are better, then comes another grief instalment. Had the relationship not been so good, the grieving wouldn't be so bad. Your deep grief is a signpost pointing to a deep lasting love connecting you to your loved one. The usual stages of grief are shock, anger, guilt, denial, depression and then a new acceptance. But everyone's grief is personal and unique.'

Declan Coyle
Author, Inspirational Speaker & Mentor

Foreword by Brian D'Arcy

Grief:

People in grief need somebody to walk with them in a non-judgmental way. This book tells a beautiful story in a down-to-earth way. It will inspire readers to journey in hope through the bereavement process. It was my privilege to visit Marian and Donald during Marian's illness, so I want to encourage you to read Donald's thoughts after all these years.

We're all familiar with the five stages of grief, originally outlined by the late Dr Elisabeth Kubler-Ross. While modern psychology has revised these stages, they still serve as a practical tool to help us begin the healing process.

Her five stages are – denial, anger, bargaining, and depression, leading hopefully, to acceptance. They are tools to help us identify what we may be feeling. They are not stops on some timeline of grief. They help us to name the emotions we experience. They assure us that we are not mad!

Henri Nouwen was a sensitive priest and insightful writer. He said that the friend who can be silent with us in a time of despair or confusion, the one who can stay with us during grief and bereavement, and who can tolerate not knowing, not healing, not curing, is a valuable friend who cares.

If you have ever experienced grief, you will understand how valuable his advice is. We should be aware that grief will consume us if we allow it to. Sometimes, a shadow of grief hangs over every part of our lives. Yet, we should not allow grief to overwhelm us because life must go on. The author C S Lewis once wrote, "I not only live each endless day in grief, I live each day thinking about living each day in grief."

The first part of grief is loss; the second is the remaking of a life. We cannot hope to regain the life we had, so we have to say good-bye to that life. However, a new life awaits us. It may be better or worse, but it is not the same life. It's hard to understand, but it's the beginning of healing once we realise that.

The way society views grieving is changing, not necessarily for the better. There is an attempt to sanitise death; people now "pass" instead of dying. No matter how society tries to avoid it, we must eventually accept that death is part of the cycle of life.
Everyone has a right and a need to grieve. Good grief is healthy grief and is personal. Each member of the same family will journey at their own pace. Husbands and wives will cope with the loss of their child in different ways.

When we lose a friend or someone we have loved deeply, we are left with grief that can paralyse us emotionally for a long time.
People we love become part of us. Our thinking, feeling, and acting are all determined by them. Our fathers, mothers, husbands, wives, lovers, children, and friends ... they live in our hearts. The result is that when they die, a part of us dies, too.

Grief is that slow and painful departure of someone who has become an intimate part of us. We feel their loss even more deeply at special times of the year - Christmas, the New Year, a birthday or an anniversary - that's when the pain becomes searing.

I believe we never 'get over' the loss of a close family member or loved one. We learn to live differently without them; we accept that life goes on even though it can never be the same. It was put to me this way: We must learn to walk well with a limp.

We don't need experts to 'take away' the grief. We don't have to be cured or healed. Healing will come in time from within. It is best to accompany them on their journey of discovery.

Different deaths bring different forms of grief. The death of an elderly person after a long illness is not the same as the death of a young person in a road accident. Suicide is different again. That's why there is no Master Plan for coping with grief. Each death needs to be acknowledged; no one lives forever. For believers, death is a gateway to a new life; death is not the end of everything. It is the end of life as we know it. We are transformed into a life of happiness that we can't imagine.

Finally, we need to be grateful. I can complain about the loss of a loved one – and I should do that – but I should be thankful for the many gifts that person brought me. In short, I should acknowledge their passing, be grateful for our shared relationship, and begin to live again without guilt. The late Cardinal Hume told us that grief is a personal journey we tread alone. It's a slow dying within, a vast emptiness, a chilling void. Silence is the best response to another's grief, he said. "Not the silence that is a pause in speech, awkward and unwanted, but one that unites heart to heart; Love, speaking in silence, is the way into the void of another's grief…

"Love comes silently and slowly to soften the pain of grief and dispel the sadness. The love of God, warm and genuine, will touch and heal the grieving heart."

Brian D'Arcy CP OBE
is an Irish Passionist priest, writer, newspaper columnist, broadcaster, and preacher. D'Arcy hosts a weekly radio programme each Sunday afternoon on BBC Radio Ulster. He is the author of several books, including A Little Bit of Religion
and A Little Bit of Healing.

<u>Contents</u>

Introduction

Welcome to the life you never wanted and to our little community who know grief well. Please take some time to introduce yourself to grief and whilst your visit is appreciated, I hope it's a short one, as no one can stay here forever. It's not where anyone belongs. There is no past or future here, we only have the present.

From here on in your days of falling victim to the cruelties the world has thrown at you is about to end, if you so desire. Even though we can't always control what happens to us, in life we are capable of making fundamental choices, which can lead us to a new and better understanding.

Our thoughts are constantly evolving and to induce healing we must be open to the possibility that we can allow new information into our minds, and with that knowledge, we can begin to build new memories. It is easy to get stuck in the past, or daydream about the future, but you can only live in the present. Now is the only reality where we can make changes either by remapping our past or planning for the future.

On my own personal journey I have had to learn how to stop avoiding and teach myself how to deal with my loss, by no longer fantasizing about what the past should have been, wishing it were different or how the future could have been. I also write these words to my younger self who would have benefitted greatly from this advice. I dedicate this book to you and your journey. Grief and loss have no respect for time and the time to face your loss is now. There's an old saying; when the pupil is ready, the teacher appears. So maybe, just maybe, this can be your opportunity.

Trying to deal with loss has a way of making our world quite literally fall apart. The fog of grief is seldom ever clearing to allow us any sense of direction. Grief is not curable as it is not an illness, even though your body tells you otherwise. You may run to avoid your grief, and procrastinate, but you cannot hide from it forever. Concepts such as 'how could they?' or 'will I ever feel whole again?' can be a struggle. Often you will appear very composed with a brave face and smile for the public, while underneath this thin veil hides your anger and brokenness that no amount of time can ever erase, whilst you are doing your best to avoid sliding into an inescapable sinkhole of quicksand with little success. I promise that if you work with me, you will achieve a level of acceptance far beyond what you would have ever thought possible.

My deepest wish for you as you read this book is that it will become a template for your knowing. This knowing is that in life all adversities carry with them the seed of an equal or better understanding, and that this understanding only reveals itself when we face what really frightens us the most. I defend your right to deal with your loss in any way that works for you. You may totally disagree with my analysis and observations, and in your defence I always say you will never get your grief story wrong. You may find it hard to believe but your grief will not stay the same. It will change, grow and recede and you will learn to be more comfortable with your story, and in time create a more meaningful life experience for yourself. Within this your loved one will somehow live on in your new narrative.

You cannot recreate the future by holding on to memories of the past. This book is about letting go of your old personal narrative and to give you the courage and tools to write a new one. I write this book with one hand in fear, the other in hope. I aim to share my personal experience to make a connection only, and not to make comparison or judgements. What I would love this book to do for you is to take you from a place of fear to a place of freedom.

In the words of one of my favourite authors (Dr Wayne Dyer) who writes:

'I see you! I see your strength and courage, your hesitations and fears. I see the way you love others and your struggle to love yourself. I see how hard you work to grow and dedication to heal. I see your vulnerable humanity and your transcendent divinity. I see you and I like what I see.'

If you simply can't understand why someone is grieving so much, for so long, then consider yourself fortunate that you do not understand. It's tempting to tell a grieving person to look to the future. What most people don't understand is that your loved one is missing in your future too. When you experience grief it's OK that you're not OK. It's OK to miss them. It's OK to cry. It's OK not to function. It's OK to be angry. It's OK to love again. It's OK to be honest. It's OK not to want to read books about grief and loss too.

Liz Newman puts it this way:

'In this life we will constantly be pulled between love and loss, grief and gratitude, pain and purpose. But how brave it is to allow yourself space for the tension to know that. Seemingly opposite experiences can be true at once and it is possible to hold them in your heart at the one time. In your grief journey you will travel at your own pace. When you finally go within, you will discover your unmissable higher self and perhaps meet this person for the very first time.'

To grieve, really grieve, takes great courage. By doing so you are allowing self-examination of your thought process and by scrutinizing your beliefs this may allow you to open yourself up the possibility that you may have to let go of many deeply held views and opinions that up until now, have held your sense of meaning together.

I admire your courage to read this book. From now on don't believe a thought you think. Your pain of loss will finally ease when you give up the hope that the past can be any different. This book is about trying to make sense as to why we suffer when we lose our nearest and dearest and struggling with an unimaginable sense of hopelessness. Let's get started, we have much to do!

This book is not intended as a road map for personal development, but hopefully you will find that it will generate thoughts and opinions that will aid you on your journey. Much of our conditioned upbringing and core beliefs were handed to us by our elders when we were young and unable to question their instruction. They in turn were relating to us what they themselves were taught. Those thoughts may have held you together until now but when you discover that your world has fallen apart then no amount of denial or regret will make the slightest difference. Death is final and you can't solve grief, but you won't always have to suffer.

Your bereavement, whether you are aware of it or not, will be a transformational experience. This book will not offer any techniques or strategies for dealing with loss, or indeed be a magic cure. On the positive side you don't have to study, remember, or do anything. This book is written in an effort to create for you a space. This space may have already existed within you and you never had the need to use it up until now, needed or wanted to think about it.

What you don't need is more information. Social media can provide endless information. What I am offering is a new fresh way of thinking about the changes that will have to take place. It is my wish that you will use this book as an aid to help you cope with the new situation you find yourself in and shine a light on a very dark road, in the knowledge that others have travelled this journey before.

Feel free to dip in and out of the pages. Hopefully some of the topics and techniques will be of interest to you, and feel free to skip other parts that are not relevant or don't fit into your way of thinking. You are under no obligation to endorse or agree, it's only my opinion and what may work for one person may not for another. My goal is simply to help those who want help.

In time you will become aware of your need to find a new normal, helping you to look at life not as it was before, but as it may unfold in the new now. In grief there is no wrong, so how can we improve from that perspective. My hope is that this book will help you shift your thinking and provide you with ideas that you might incorporate into your new experience of discovering your higher self.

When you find this higher self, you will be able to stay in the moment and learn to trust your own innate wisdom. You will no longer be looking to others for changes you want to make in your life. Your struggle with self-doubt and indecision will give way to a clearer understanding of what you need to do to rebuild your life. The absolute truths that you once held may have to be amended to enable you to learn and trust your new higher self and innate wisdom to support your new reality.

Some days you won't be able to be normal, some days you will avoid showing your broken heart. Some days you will travel through this journey very slowly and at your own pace. The love you still have for what you have lost will make you write a new narrative for yourself, and I encourage you to physically write down your thoughts on paper because it will matter more than you think. In time you will look back to your writing to see how far you have come in your journey. You may keep your notes or decide it's time to let them go. As I have said, in grief, you will never get it wrong.

My Heart:
My heart
In all its brokenness
Will always look for you
Chasing down
A familiar scent
Following the trail
Of a favourite memory,
Relentless in its pursuit.
Every morning,
Feeling the ache
Of that now familiar wound
Of navigating a life, a story
Whose chapters were too few.
But, what a legacy you've left
In the chapters you were here,
And what a story that you've left
A love that perseveres.

My heart
In all its hopefulness
Will always look for you
Cherishing these
Sometimes painful memories,
Holding them tightly
To feel you with me too.
Your absence brings
A deep and lingering ache
But your love
Persists here too,
A bond that will never break
That will comfort and continue.
So, it seems
No matter what I do,
My heart will always look for you.

In everything I do.
In every memory, old and new.
My heart will always look for you.

(Liz Newman)

From grief to joy - How new beginnings can become disguised as painful endings:

The cost of loving means to be open to constant change and when we let go insisting that nothing must change only then will we discover what we might become. It is only by breaking out of our grief and life of bondage, by accepting the flaws in ourselves and others that we can begin to see light at the end of the tunnel.

Events, even tragic events, carry with them the kernel of opportunity to grow in the experience of an uncertain life. You can stop crying and continue grieving. People can say you're doing better today and to them and the outside world you are doing better. However you can wake every day knowing that your loved one is not here or ever coming back, and grief can be hard to explain. All I know is I will miss you today and I don't know what tomorrow will bring but I know I will miss you. Our challenge is to let go of what we were to discover what we might become. It's OK to only do the minimum and to keep going. Just remember we have the choice to make the rest of life the best of life.

Grief is a living thing and you may try to avoid it but it returns at will. You can do your best to avoid or numb it by indulging in excessive alcohol, drugs, taking unnecessary risks, by forming toxic relationships, excessive working, anything to avoid facing reality. The fact is your grief will wait until you finish so you might as well let it show up in whatever form and deal with it. Never apologise for your tears or feelings of helplessness. We come into this world with nothing and leave pretty much the same way, with nothing. Our quest and goal in life is to discover self-love, because if we don't, we suffer in the absence of self-love. When we don't love ourselves we are going to have a difficult time loving anybody. Just try to find something to focus on. Don't lose yourself in your task but stay at something that distracts you from your pain and give it your undivided attention until the thought subsides at least a little. Compose your feelings and allow your bearable/pleasant thoughts to begin to outnumber those of your loss.

The following tips may help you cope with extreme negative thinking and feelings of desperation, maybe not now but in the future. We can easily convince ourselves that nothing really matters now. This can be a far cry from the person who would normally demand perfection in themselves and others. These see-saw emotions can, if unchecked and allowed to flourish, lead us into a state of anxiety and undermine our ability to make good clear choices. Always allow time and space for self-care at every stage of your grief. Just remember the grief you shared was worth it. It is worthwhile grieving every day, including many long, lonely nights. It is worth the hurt knowing they will never return and not being able to hold them. No matter how much pain we feel, not ever knowing them and their essence and joy they brought into our lives is worse. The greater the pain the more an effect that person had on our lives when they were with us. By not grieving we are trying to ignore that part of our life. Sometimes we have to grieve twice. We can feel two sets of grief. One is our own pain grieving and missing them from the moment they left and the other is everything they are missing by not being in our future.

Berne Brown advises when supporting a grieving person:

'Don't look away from people in pain. Don't look down. Don't pretend not to see hurt. Look people in the eye even when their pain is overwhelming, and when you are in pain find the people who can look you in the eye. We need to know we are not alone, especially when we are hurting.'

Chapter One
Marian's story.

If you are reading this book to support someone, I thank you for your compassion and your talent. Never underestimate the power of your presence, a kind non-judgemental word or an honest compliment. You must be willing to hold space for someone else. By holding space, I mean that you are willing to walk alongside another person and sometimes get into their muddy puddle in whatever journey they are on. Remember not to judge them or make them feel inadequate. Don't try to fix them or affect the outcome of their journey. When we hold space for another person, we open our hearts, offer support, and let go of judgement and control.

When you listen, try to really listen and understand. You do not always have to respond. You don't need to have all the answers, sometimes just listening is what the person speaking needs. When we are talking with the bereaved, insofar as we can, we must try to suspend our own judgements and preconceived notions of how people should behave, especially when they trust you enough to confide in you at this difficult time in their life. Always remember we can lose someone in an instant and grieve their loss for a lifetime.

Grief never ends because the love you had never ends. What has to end is the feelings of misplaced trauma and sense of desolation. Your grief belongs to you, and you are allowed to feel the loss, fear, anger, sadness and be overwhelmed. In your grief you must be allowed to do whatever feels right for you and not what society expects.

Declan Forde speaking at Marian's funeral. St Mary's Church, Killyclogher, Omagh, 9/11/2000

'It's hard to believe and accept that Marian will soon lie beneath the falling leaves of Autumn camouflaged by her own colours of gold, yellow, brown, and russet. I can only give you my measure of the Marian I was privileged and honoured to know. Open yet private, quiet, yet laughing, petite, every inch a lady, religious in a true spiritual way, humble, yet intensely proud of her family, smiling friendly, honest, and truly gentle and loving, and loved.
She was a gentle fighter, she wrestled with her angel of Death, but defied and kept him at bay with two simple weapons, the will to live and will to love. To be given love is a gift, but to really give and share love, that is the greatest gift of all.
Here today we are showing Marian our simple gift of love. She touched all of us and what a special gift we each received from her. Thank you, Marian, for the person you were in our memories. Thank you for the person you are in our tears and thank you for the person you will always be in our hearts.'

When Marian passed away I thought I was going to be forever in a dark place, but in hindsight I was planted. I read somewhere a quote that in life all adversities carry with them the seed of an equal or better experience. I found this an extremely difficult concept to accept as a universal truth. Two decades later I have found that it is true. However no one likes their world and sense of place to be torn apart. We are faced with choices on how we are going to deal with our loss and how to rebuild our lives in meaningful ways.

Writing about my personal relationship with Marian and our journey together, even after all this time, has been extremely difficult for me. I have reopened my personal grief story not for any other reason other than to make a connection to you the reader. In the early days of my grief I would never have shared my experience.

However with the passing of time, self-examination and listening to countless more tragic losses, I realise that sharing our most difficult experiences has both personal risks and a huge potential for allowing our minds to make sense of our losses. I lacked the courage to open up to anyone about my feelings which resulted in me making my life and others close to me very difficult and stunting my progression in the process.

This story about Marian is messy, it is chaotic and will remain unfinished because I don't know what my grief may look like tomorrow. Even after all these years, such is the nature of loss. The love we hold for those we have lost is so deeply important to us. The chapters of their love are turned by the pages of our memoirs and are always ours to keep. Our grief stories and how they come to be written belong to us and us alone. I share my story to help you narrate your own. When you can write about your loss it can help you navigate through your journey and don't worry about what everyone else is going to say or think. Write it for yourself and don't allow the judgements of others stop you from you becoming a better version of yourself.

I have worked for more years than I care to remember in bereavement support and this is what inspired me to write this book about grief and loss. Have you ever settled down to watch a film and the storytelling starts at the end emphasizing that the real story is about the journey? This portion of the book is about my journey. As a bereavement support worker/counsellor I have had the honour and privilege to accompany many people on their own personal journeys as we discussed how their bereavement resulted in our paths crossing. I have learned that the universe doesn't do accidental and the people we meet have come into our lives either for a reason or season. When clients present themselves for bereavement support, they are taking a major step in opening up about their loss and will only do so on the understanding that any and all conversations are totally private and confidential. I could write books longer than *'War and Peace'* about what clients have said to me over the years. I have been privileged beyond words to sit with clients as together we try to make sense of the 'what' and 'how' their loss has affected them. I would never betray any of their confidences. The only person I am going to discuss in this book, or use examples of, is from my own experiences and my story.

I first met Marian, who was to become my future wife and mother to our children, on the first of January 1972. We met at a dance in the Gap Ballroom when we had just turned seventeen years of age. Asking a stranger out to dance was not an easy thing to do. Those were the days when ladies were expected to line up against the wall and men would walk up and down looking for someone suitable to dance with. It was nothing short of a human cattle market, humiliating for both sexes, the woman for not being approached and the risk of being turned down for the men, walking away with a feeling of total rejection.

It was my good fortune to ask Marian out and as she took my hand I discovered it was a slow set of about three or four songs; long enough for us both to decide to head upstairs for a lemonade, and I asked to escort her home. She politely refused because she was only allowed to go to the dance on the understanding that she went home with her older sister. But we made a date to meet at the same venue the following Sunday.

Over forty-five years later I can still remember exactly what she was wearing the night we met. I can still see her pale, unblemished complexion and her white mini dress and black leather boots. I was wearing twenty-six-inch bell bottoms and a green velvet jacket, brown platform boots with long brown shoulder length hair, which I assure you was the height of fashion at the time. I had just purchased my first car, a green Volkswagen Beetle and recently left school for my first job.

We met during the height of what we called the 'Troubles' in Northern Ireland and for our own safety we did not travel far from home, so our social life centred around local venues and dances, sometimes in glorified canvas tents in neighbouring parishes called carnivals. During these times the Church and State had power and a vested interest in keeping everyone segregated and we were encouraged to fear meeting any strangers outside our own community. This may have been the time of flower power and free love but sadly didn't filter down to our rural Omagh in Co Tyrone. You were expected to refrain from the sins of the flesh with fear and guilt-tripping the tools to keep us in line and like many others who were emotionally blackmailed, duly observed. This was a time when society would have expected you to settle down and marry in your early twenties. Looking back, I think of the social pressure on young adults, not long out of the childhood experience themselves.

We got engaged on Halloween in 1975 with a day trip to Jameson's of Henry Street in Dublin, and such a joy to experience the novelty of being allowed into a shop without being searched. We planned a short engagement and soon afterwards set a date for September 1977 for our wedding on the way home. We were given half an acre of land from my father and began to plan to build our home. Planning a wedding and preparing to build a house at twenty-one years of age meant we both had to forgo any further dances and concentrate on work picking up an extra part-time job to raise much needed funds. Unfortunately like most young people of our generation we could not burden our parents with the cost of a wedding with both of us finding extra work to help cover the expense. Anyway, we married on the 17th of September 1977 and work was well underway on our home, a long apex bungalow typical of 1977 architecture. Sadly, my father, who was only fifty-five years of age, was diagnosed with terminal lung cancer while we were on our honeymoon. He passed away six weeks later. My brother and I sat with our dad the night before his death and in one of his more lucid moments he told me if only I had known how much I was loved. I held his hand and I watched as he passed away early the next morning.

We moved into our bungalow in May 1978 and immediately tried to have a family. Months of disappointment led to us contacting our GP and an onward referral to a gynaecologist who diagnosed endometriosis and blocked fallopian tubes leaving the possibility of conceiving greatly reduced but not impossible, and so we were discharged and told to just hope for the best. At that time there was little or no support for infertility except by going private. If you are aware of how the infertility process was back then, then you will know exactly how humiliating the system is. We were pretty-much left in the lap of the Gods and after a further two years decided to make an application to adopt.

Of all the decisions we can make in our lives this was by far the best one we ever made, and four years later we adopted our first child, a boy Jonathan. Four years after that we were blessed again with our second adoption and our second child, a daughter Maria. There is an old English proverb that says 'blood is thicker than water,' in other words blood relations and family bonds are always stronger that other relationships. This is just another one of the many sayings that people use without any realisation of their ignorance, and are quick to adapt as some sort of set-in-stone remark. Another one that comes to mind is 'you made your bed so you can lie in it', meaning you must accept the unpleasant results of something you may have later regretted. People will use these and similar infallible quotes that are well past their sell-by date. Well-meaning people are quick to quote these saying in the absence of not having anything encouraging or constructive to say.

Both Jonathan in 1981 and Maria in 1985 were only three months old when placed into our care and then the lengthy proceedings to make the adoption formal. In all honesty Marian and I never experienced greater love and felt truly blessed when our children arrived. She only used the words 'just perfect' four times in our relationship. The first was when she chose her engagement ring, and the next two utterances when seeing the children for the first time. The words *just perfect* were never used lightly as I was to find out many years later.

In those days it was a mandatory adoption rule that the mother relinquishes her job and becomes a full-time stay-at-home mother. Interest rates were spiralling out of all control and her leaving a well-paid, secure job was a challenge, and sometimes necessity is the mother of invention. To supplement our income, I got a job as a DJ in a local nightclub which later on developed into hiring out PA sound systems. This made up for any shortfall in our income. We were truly happy and blessed having two beautiful children, a decent home and health and happiness in abundance. We bought our first new car and a mobile holiday home in Donegal. If I learned anything in life is that nothing stays the same for too long, either good or bad.

The years joyously passed quickly, our children were in primary school, and we were then told that only two adopted children could be placed in any one home. Earlier we had been to see a private consultant gynaecologist who was treating Marian for her infertility and we both wanted one last chance for another child before her natural childbirth window closed. She was booked into the Royal Victoria Hospital in Belfast a few days before Easter (1990) for a small procedure to remove a small ovarian cyst which would then aid the IVF process. I had taken a few days annual leave to look after the children and on the morning of the operation the phone rang. As usual I had Van Morrison on and couldn't hear what the voice was saying on the phone. When I turned the music off, I could hear the consultant's voice and from his tone he sounded very serious. He said he was ringing from the operating theatre and instead of a small operation he was going to perform a complete hysterectomy as he was convinced that she had ovarian cancer and it was necessary for her survival. He said it was important that I be at her bedside when she would awake to explain the situation. He told me that there would be further procedures, and he would talk to us when he was free.

One minute I was blissfully listening to music and the next trying to pack some of the children's clothes to stay with their granny, as I made my way to the hospital. From memory it was a living nightmare. As I drove up the motorway, I was trying to think what I was going to say to Marian and how I could break the news that not only had she lost any hope of having another child, but that her life was in serious danger.

When I arrived at the hospital, I was told that the doctor had gone home and the ward sister took me into her office. She didn't have to say much as I could read her body language and spotted a hidden tear in the corner of her eye. Marian was still very sedated and I sat by her bed, but I remember that every five minutes or so I was going to the bathroom to try and compose my thoughts and dry my tears. As the anaesthetic began to wear off, she was groggy and complained about the pain. I told her that the doctors decided it was in her best interests to remove all her reproductive organs as they were suspicious, but until the lab results came back they were not certain. Marian could always read me like a book and before falling into an induced sleep said, *'Don't tell me this is malignant, please don't.'*

The instructions the surgeon gave me on our telephone call reminded me it was my duty to 'inform your wife and she must know the truth.' She was in hospital for Easter but was released the following Wednesday and she insisted we have our Easter lunch and chocolate eggs with our children when she came home. A few weeks later Marian had her first round of chemo and while the sickness was debilitating to say the least it was the losing of her hair that had the most traumatic effect. Women never really think about hair loss until they face losing it. For women, hair loss can be a sign to the world that you have cancer and Marian was very private about sharing this information with others and was fortunate to have a very good hairdresser and friend to assist with this distressing side effect.

Marian and I had to try to keep life as normal as possible for our young children and wrestle with the knowledge that on top of never having any more children her life expectation was very much in the lap of the Gods. After the first treatment she was called for routine check-ups and we talked at length about how we might manage her illness. Her thoughts were solely for our children and their welfare. Marian was very religious in a true sense of the word and did her best to accept what life had thrown at us. Here we were, a young couple in our mid-thirties bargaining with a God that she was taught to love and trust, to be allowed the gift of life to see her children grown. I remember her waking up one night and telling me I need at least ten years to get our children to some level of independence. If I get that I won't complain. We decided that from that day on we would never stare into an empty grave and instead devote ourselves to keeping life as normal as possible.

Soon after we sold our static mobile home and bought a new touring caravan. We toured Ireland, heading down the west coast and up via Dublin in the east. Every three months we would have to make the journey to the hospital for checkups and almost to the day, two years after her first diagnosis, the doctor said she needed more surgery as the cancer had returned. He arranged for her to be re-admitted for surgery a week later. Leaving the hospital that afternoon I thought my legs would not carry me. All Marian could say was why would the God she adored give her two beautiful children and not allow her to see them grow up. Some short time later she had major surgery and was placed in the high dependency ward. I remember being allowed in to see her and she was pale and wrapped in tinfoil blanket to keep her body warm. The new tumour had attached itself to her bowel and her bladder, she now had a colostomy bag attached and had to endure a lot of pain, but in her true spiritual acceptance she got herself home and prepared for a second bout of chemo with the usual sickness and hair loss. Being home we tried to get some sort of order into our lives again and our children's lives as they were oblivious to what their mother was going through. My faith was tested. I wondered how when at this time of great Christian joy, God would somehow crucify us again. Marian's way of dealing with this was that she was just going to do what it takes to get well again. Along with the chemo she required at least fifteen sessions of radiotherapy. We went weekly to Belvoir Park Hospital and the chemo, along with the radiotherapy, really took its toll, but in her true fashion of wonderful bravery and a positive outlook the final scans looked quite promising, and we just got on with our lives.

Marian placed her faith in God, and we did our best to rebuild our lives. We had both turned forty that year and did not feel like parties or any outward sign of celebration so I gave her a nice diamond ring and she gave me a Rolex and a card saying this is an expensive watch but not near as precious as the time we might have. We knew that our time as a family was going to be limited and so we had little time for any trivial arguments and kept things as normal as possible for our children. They were our world, and we made sure that our worries and troubles were not going to add to theirs. Maria always wanted to visit Disneyland. I knew that Marian's deteriorating health issues were not going to allow us this type of holiday and tried to have special holidays closer to home.

At the end of the summer Marian began to complain about feeling unwell and having lower back pain. We went back to our consultant who felt it could be another tumour and after a few tests he unfortunately was correct in his assessment. This time he was not sure if she would survive such major surgery and we were referred to the Belfast City Hospital. Some of the doctors had suggested to let nature take its course but Marian was keen to have more surgery to buy her some time. The operation took place early on a Monday morning and for eight hours they did their best to remove the tumour. That night I got in to see her in the intensive care ward and all I could see was this pale, fragile shadow strapped to monitors. As I held her hand she said, *'Am I alive?'* I patted her hand reassuring her she was very much alive. *'Are you sure? I am so glad,'* she said as she drifted into unconsciousness.

Her consultant was not overly optimistic and said by removing the tumour he had managed to buy us some time. After three weeks in the high dependency ward Marian was discharged home again. By this time Jonathan was in the middle of his A-levels and we both tried to concentrate on his exams and keep things in the family as normal as possible. Marian was able to purchase a good quality hairpiece and managed to put on a little weight. The next few months were wonderful and life was good. Marian had been ironing clothes one day when she said her back was sore. We both put it down to the fact that she had been standing too long in the one location. A few days later she felt sick and we put it down to the lingering effects of the chemo. To be on the safe side we had another scan and biopsy and had to wait in hospital for three days for the result. I arrived at the hospital and again was ushered into the consultant's waiting room. The staff nurse said, *'I am sorry to tell you that we just got a call to say that Marian's father, who was in hospital in Dungannon at the time, has died suddenly.'* They knew I was on my way so thought it would be better for me to tell her the news.

Marian just wanted to be with her family, and we were preparing to get her dressed when the consultant came in. He sympathized with Marian on the loss of her father adding that he had more bad news. The biopsy was malignant, and he suggested as it was the first of December, we should have Christmas at home and return to hospital in the New Year or alternatively stay in hospital for Christmas. Marian just wanted to be with her family, and we opted to go home and return after Christmas. We both knew we were running out of options and without discussion knew that this would be our last Christmas. We referred back to our promise not to stare into the empty grave and made the most of that Christmas. Marian spent it by bringing in the new millennium with her family while I was working as I was unable to get cover.

January arrived and we found ourselves back in the City Hospital again. Marian was prepared for surgery and we both knew this was our last opportunity. During the surgery I spent most of the time in prayer in the little hospital chapel and tried to take a walk about the grounds. When I returned to the ward, I was surprised to find Marian back and sleeping. She didn't have the expected usual post operation apparatus attached. The doctor came up to our bed while Marian was still in a very deep sleep. He removed his surgical mask and I could see from his expression that we were now in the end game. He said Marian had a large mast tumour which was inoperable. He wouldn't give a time frame but said it would be over quite soon. He was referring us to palliative care and would recommend admission to the hospice.

He left and continued his rounds and chatted with the other patients. I made a quick temporary exit for fear that Marian would wake up and I didn't want to break down in front of her, and needed to gather my thoughts. I had often, during her illness, felt totally alone and unable to share my thoughts, but this was the mother of them all. When she began to wake up from her sedation the look on my face probably said it all and she asked me if the operation was successful. I said that the doctors are now going to manage the illness with drugs and the doctors would be having a chat with us when she was well enough to receive them and with that she fell back into a deep sleep again.

I could feel the atmosphere in the ward change as the doctors passed our bed and didn't stop. I overhead a junior doctor say to his friend this patient has been referred to palliative care. I couldn't bring myself to tell her and invented a half-truth and said the doctors thought that it was unsafe to try to remove the tumour and would be recommending a high dose of radiation to shrink it before trying to remove it. She looked at me and said, *'what was the junior doctor saying about palliative care?'* I replied that sometimes patients are referred there for pain management, but she didn't buy my explanation. She asked the nurse to have her consultant call and explain the situation.

To his credit he called and said that the operation was not possible. He had referred her to another consultant who would be treating her from now on as his role in our journey was over. He squeezed her hand and left. A few hours later we were introduced to another consultant and he was more positive and stated that as Marian had reacted well to chemo and radiation in the past that in his view this would be our best option. We were soon discharged into the care of our local hospital in Omagh for blood transfusions and pain management.

We were told that Macmillan nurses would be calling to support us, but Marian said she wanted me to nurse her at home and with the help of family and friends we respectfully declined their offer. Our GP called my mobile and arranged for me to call for a chat. When I arrived at the surgery he was reading Marian's file. I broke down and said I can't bring myself to tell her we are at the end stage. He responded by telling me I didn't have to as she already knows and is well aware. When I got home, I tried to explain that we were at the end stage now and she looked at me and said, *'I don't want to discuss this.'* But we both knew what was on the cards without going into any great detail.

A home care plan was put in place and I took a career break from work. As she requested, I nursed her and cared for her every need, as we would have done with our children. When the carers would call, I would have her showered, the commode used and emptied and had her pain relief sorted before they arrived. Her dear mother had moved in to help us and we kept things as normal as possible. We spent some months with her in a hospital bed with help from support carers and going back and forth to our local hospital for additional pain relief and blood transfusions. Marian began to lose weight and was often sick and we both, without talking in any detail, knew we had no options left. Our GP had suggested Marian go to the hospice in Belfast and I was surprised that she agreed. I had to try to find a form of words to explain to Jonathan and Maria. When I spoke to Jonathan he went into a state of denial and Maria, like her granny, turned to prayer.

We arrived at the hospice on a beautiful spring afternoon when the daffodils were in bloom and the first signs of spring after the long winter and yet something inside me was so cold and I couldn't make sense of how life was so normal for everyone else as ours was imploding. Marian had a nice room and was well treated, and I was allowed to have a reclining chair next to her bed. Late one evening we had the conversation I dreaded as I knew that when we would have this conversation, we could never go back to not having it. I asked her was there anything she wanted us to do for her and she requested no long farewells and get her hair and make-up done before you close my coffin. Just do what you need to do, and it will be fine. She held my hand and said I hope you meet someone nice.

Next morning a most beautiful handmade get-well card for Marian arrived from Maria. In her innocence she obviously didn't understand the gravity of the situation. Jonathan had got accepted to university in Belfast and he and a friend were looking for a house to rent. Marian announced to the nurse that she needed to go home and she would be leaving the hospice that afternoon and had me help her get dressed. Off we went to Omagh but not before heading into Belfast to have a look at Jonathan's student accommodation.

The next morning, I nipped into town for a few groceries and when I came home Marian was at the kitchen sink and the pump for her IV drugs was lying on the kitchen table. She stated that she didn't need these just yet because they were making her sleepy and that it was her body which she knew best. Much to the surprise of our doctor and the nurses she managed another seven months without the need for IV drugs. While she was very weak, had little appetite and spent the majority of her time in bed, she was still very much aware of her surroundings.

I was sent to Omagh to get Maria her new school uniform which Marian inspected from her bed and after several slight changes it got her approval. Jonathan had just moved away from home and was settling down at university. Marian began vomiting small amounts of blood and our doctor became concerned that she may have a major haemorrhage and prepared me that if this was the case her end would be traumatic and to have plenty of towels at hand.

She became so weak that she was unable to walk and with her weight loss I could quite comfortably lift her, and indeed did carry her around the house like a young child when required. All she was managing was high calorie drinks, some custard and water. The next day I overheard her on the phone to my sister who is a beautician making an appointment to have her eyebrows done. That was her last journey and on the way home we passed by our local church and cemetery. She said in a low tone, *'this is where I will be coming to soon.'* I didn't answer and I knew she had finished trying to survive.

Two days after that she stopped drinking and eating and I carried her to bed for the last time, like a parent would carry a young child. I rang her family and said that I didn't think Marian would be with us very much longer. They gathered at our home and we, as in the Catholic tradition, lit candles and said some prayers. She grew very weak, and her voice was just above a whisper. I held her hand and I knew despite her eyes closing she could see someone or something and her breathing was laboured.

She gently squeezed my hand and spoke her last words. She said, *'It's just perfect.'* I didn't understand what she was saying but she repeated it again and I knew what she meant. I replied, 'We'll go now and we will meet again,' and with that she breathed her last breath and passed away.

We sat quietly and I held her, and we didn't speak. There was such peacefulness and relief that her pain and suffering was over but for me it was like a trap door opening and a whole different reality was waiting for me.

The finality of death is that it never changes. You may change and life will change but death is so final. Marian passed away in the early hours of the morning. Jonathan was in Belfast and Maria was asleep. I arranged for Jonathan to be collected and taken home as I didn't want him to drive the journey on his own. I gently awoke Maria before calling the doctor and undertaker. I could see the pain of Marian's passing etched in the faces of her mother and her family as they mumbled their final prayers as she slipped away. I knew her time had come, and it was her time to leave. We all knew that we had lost a beautiful soul.

In a matter of a few moments Marian was gone. Her lifeless body was prepared for her wake and I watched family and friends prepare our home. I remember cowering in my sitting room as the undertakers came with her coffin as our rooms were cleared out to make-way for visitors to our home. I remember I wanted to put something on the hall floor to protect the light coloured carpet from the countless feet that would be walking into our home in the next few days. How some trivial thought can invade your mind as your world falls apart. I have since learned this is not that uncommon and nothing more than our mind finding distractions to avoid facing the avalanche of unwanted reality. I felt the feeling of euphoria and at the same time a loss that could never be put into words. Her suffering was now over and the realisation that there is dignity in death soon gave way to a terrifying realisation that I was now on my own in this world and she would stay frozen in time as my life would have to move on alone in my journey.

There is much divided opinion on the ritual of wakes and their place in the twenty-first century. My opinion would be that in Ireland we have, or at least had, a good mechanism for allowing our neighbours and friends to come into our homes and allow the grieving family to meet, talk and share fond memories while making good any disputes. Repeating the story of our loved ones helps enormously to make the sense of loss more real as only by repeating and remembrance can we begin to comprehend the finality of our loss.

Three days later we brought Marian to her funeral Mass where she was laid to rest in our new family grave. All her life Marian dreaded being in a confined space and I really struggled with lowering the coffin into the soil. She detested MRI scanners and I would have to wear protective garments and hold her feet with the promise I would pull her out immediately if the claustrophobia became unbearable. Unfortunately on this occasion I could not help her but I remember well whispering to her a very personal message reassuring her that it's going to be OK.

As friends and family shook my hand someone who I didn't know or recognise from behind my back put a large hand on my shoulder with tremendous pressure and almost pushed me into the ground. They never spoke to me but it was a great feeling because it grounded me again. We made our way to the Church hall for refreshments and the mood changed from being sombre to soft yet pleasant sounds of people in light conversations. One by one people left the hall and I became so engrossed that for a moment I looked around to see where Marian was to take her home too. That was the first moment of realisation that I was now on my own. My title had changed from husband to widower.

Over the weeks the apparatus that supported Marian was removed, the wheelchair, hospital bed, commode and countless other items were consigned to the garage and were collected and dispatched for some other person in need of them. I returned to work in a few days as work was my only distraction and I made myself busy as a way of distracting me from the pain of my grief. I learned that you can try to avoid grief but grieving will wait, it has endless patience. Where is God when it hurts this much, I thought to myself. The agony of grief is total and I was taken to the edge of despair. While Marian was resting in peace my whole reason for living was gone. She was not only missing in my past but in my future too.

It's amazing how after the funeral people go back to their normal lives and there I was lost at sea. I am sure, because her passing was expected, family and friends would have thought that I had somehow managed to prepare myself. Marian and I had during her illness made a pact that no matter how difficult things were we would never look into the empty grave. In other words, we wouldn't give any thought to her not being around. This was a wonderful coping mechanism at the time but when the reality finally arrived it was something I never gave any serious consideration about. As far as I was concerned I was suddenly a widower.

The support systems put in place for Marian's well-being and spiritual support didn't include me or our children. Our wonderful priest, after the funeral, never called nor any of the medical team who were so constant in our home for the last few months of her life. I understand it's not possible with the health care system and churches struggling to cope with the pressure of demands but as a society we need to support the bereaved. On a personal level I was too proud to seek help and saw my inability to cope as some sort of weakness that I wouldn't want others to witness. The last thing I would have asked for was support from a bereavement support worker as, in my mind, how could anyone know how I was really feeling. No disrespect to any well-meaning volunteer but the thought of it would have me running to the hills.

In my fixed logic I suffered alone for many years by becoming a workaholic and avoiding doing the self-examination required to help make sense of our individual ways of grieving. My appeal to anyone reading this today is to reach out to anyone you can trust with your feelings. It may not be family or friends because often the ones who love you the most are so emotionality invested in your story that they can't really find the words that you may need to hear. This is not dissimilar to not being able to teach your children to drive a car. It's often best left to an instructor as you are too close to your child to give them impartial advice.I found myself widowed and the term was uncomfortable for me to describe.

In a few weeks the sympathy cards began to dwindle and family and friends who would have called in the days and weeks after soon began to diminish. I found myself totally alone on New Year's Eve night as I didn't want to be around people and dampen their celebrations. I watched as the year ebbed away and as the chiming clock ushered in the New Year I knew that this year had finally ended and with it had gone my world. I thought back to the New Year's night in 1972 when we first met and the excitement of falling in love with joyful anticipation as we began to build our dreams.

Over a long number of years I have learned that if we have one thought on the past and the other on the future then we miss the present, and that is what it is - a present. It should not to be squandered on worry about what has happened or what might happen in the future. For me I felt the end had come too fast. I needed more time to process the loss. I needed a thousand tomorrows and countless more 'I love yous' before allowing her memory to leave.

Marian's passing ended a life, not a relationship. All the love we created was still there and grief is love with no form of expression. In the early days of grief we cannot imagine that there's going to be any such feeling other than knowing that I am never going to see her again. In time I learned to soften and in her absence, amid coping with bouts of incredible sadness, I struggled on. In the beginning it may seem impossible but grief does have a pattern. It has a beginning, middle and something like an end (which is actually more like a new beginning). It's through the brokenness of our hearts that they enter like a chink of light breaking the darkness and we can begin to sense a feeling of warmth and closeness. If we choose we can, out of love and respect, allow ourselves to rebuild our lives in new and meaningful ways.

Death is terrible, but not as terrible as you think. You might not want to think about death, but like all of life's inevitabilities, death is very much a part of our meaning structure. We know that it will come around and we know it will hurt. We are never prepared for the pain and destruction of having our lives pulled up by the roots, our core beliefs challenged and our sense of meaning structure obliterated. Our story is the glue that holds us together. By becoming unstuck and having everything we took for granted shattered whilst having to face the prospect of creating a new life story is unimaginable. You are in crisis and see no way of making things better. There are no solutions.

In Chinese Mandarin the word for crisis means *'an opportunity riding on a dangerous wind.'* Every challenge is an opportunity for personal growth. I respect your pain, and the way you express it. I know you cry, and you will cry without comfort. Maybe you think that things will never get better but you will get stronger.

Chapter Two
Coping with loss and the potential self-damage of not dealing with it.

Scott Peck, in his famous book, *'The Road Less Travelled'*, opens with the line *'Life is difficult.'* In life we are going to lose our family and friends. It is not a matter of if, but when that grief will make its way into our lives and if you are reading this book then there is a good chance that this experience has already happened to you. During your life you are going to lose your mother, you are going to lose your father, you are going to lose children, friends, people and animals that you love. It is going to happen. You are going to experience hurt, pain and lose money. Friends and individuals are going to hurt you. Some people may just walk out of your life without explanation leaving you to wonder what you did wrong. If you spend your time waiting for the world to be the way you want it to be, refusing any opportunity to make new choices, then you are going to live a life of endless fear, blame and helpless frustration.

This book is about creating your own constructive reality because we create what we believe. This at first may feel like bad news because in the words of Wayne Dyer, *'We become what we think about.'* *In one of his lectures he described it this way; 'If you squeeze oranges what comes out?'* The answer is obviously orange juice but what he was demonstrating was that whatever is inside us comes out under pressure. As humans we are unable to stop these unwanted events happening but on the flip side, we can decide how we are going to cope with them. It is our decision to allow the tragedies that befall us in life to either make or break us. The final decision is always ours and if we embrace change, even of our most deeply held convictions, and remove the temptation for blame then we can rebuild our lives in imaginative ways for the better. We must find creative ways to cope with life's challenges and be open to question our previously held beliefs.

Finding meaning in death (Meaning Structure):

The Jesuits in the Catholic Church say, 'Show me the child and you can have the adult for life. I was born Catholic, so I have an A level in guilt.' (Billy Connolly)

Our inherited beliefs are probably responsible for our major triggers, and we automatically go back to these core values and make adult decisions without really questioning our beliefs and how we got them. If I could suggest you make a list of your own core beliefs that were given to you before the age of ten years or so. Begin with your parents, teachers, Church, society friends or anyone who had influence over you as a young child. Now begin to ask yourself if these are really your own true beliefs or were they imparted to you by these significant others, who were just passing on what they were given to them as children? We can see a cycle of inherited beliefs going back generations, some good and some not so good.

We have the power to identify these and break the chain for the better. Look closely at those people who gave you these personal set of rules and consider how their lives may have been different had they had access to a different belief set. If you are fortunate, many, if not all, may have been a positive experience, but I would guess most would be a mixture of positive and negative. Some of our core childhood values have stood us in good stead and have been useful and important signposts to guide us in our journey. If and when you decide to free yourself from what I would call the 'just world view beliefs', then you will be amazed at how these heavily inherited beliefs no longer hold you back.

As long as we continue to live and be aware we will grapple with loss. It will show its face in many facets throughout our lives. As children we may experience the loss of our beloved pets, and during our teenage years we may face the experience of having our heart broken in romances. Later we may have the experience of a broken marriage or long-term relationships. We can and will, during our lives, experience countless loss scenarios. We can lose our job for example, a place that for many of us gives us meaning and dignity. Of all the losses that living can expose us to, by far the greatest is loss through bereavement. As we rapidly approach twenty-five years into the new millennium, due to the society we live in we are very much unprepared and ill-equipped to be able to confront the reality of death and our own mortality.

In a world filled with social media and *'Doctor Google'* we know too well that death is inevitable. Death is very much a taboo subject and a constant reminder of our personal vulnerability. The thought of dying can leave us frightened and we will at all costs avoid the discussion whenever possible. However, if we have the courage and foresight to grapple with loss and not hide from its inevitability we can find rich rewards and avoid much pain in our lives and that of our families. (When fear knocks at the door and faith answers, no one is there). Society and social media influence us to believe that we are unique and irreplaceable but at the same time we are not immortal. So on a human level we walk a duel pathway alone as travellers through life, each with our own interpretation, always guessing with no one knowing enough to be certain. We can project and display signs that it couldn't happen to me, but it can and it will. It is not a matter of if, but when.

We will try and avoid these possibilities and hope that these experiences will happen to others but never to us. One of our best coping mechanisms for loss is anger. Unfortunately in Western society people with a religious view are not supposed to show this emotion. Religion teaches us that some benign spirit is directing our lives for our higher good and whatever comes our way, we should not question it. It is supposed to be unbecoming of a good religious person to question the will of God. Did Jesus not cry out during his crucifixion '*My God my God why have you forsaken me?*' The loss experience will leave us angry and if not recognised will cause emotional, physical and psychological damage.

Sometimes in extreme cases, unexpressed anger can be turned inwards and can leave us at risk of self-harm. Anger felt by the bereaved can be an extension of the anger felt by the dying person with the terminal prognosis. Sometimes the anger is turned on God and who better to blame, after all is He not supposed to be responsible for the set-up.

How often have you witnessed some horrific event and asked how could this good, kind and loving God allow such loss to take place. With this outrage can come a feeling of guilt for we are taught by the Christian Church never to question God's will in our lives. Modern religious leaders now understand that this cry from the heart is just a human response from the broken-hearted, and we are just finite beings trying to understand infinite reality. We have few answers for the broken-hearted trying to deal with tragic loss in our supposedly just world. You don't just lose someone once. You lose them every morning when you wake up. There is no end to this loss. We can only learn how not to drown when the waves of grief wash over you unexpectedly when you realise that your loved one is gone forever.

In time grief will be replaced by tender moments of memories. When we lose someone our entire landscape must change. Our long term plans we had with our loved one must adapt to this new single outlook on life. We grieve not only for the person but for the loss of the shared hopes and dreams now never to be realized. Their love has still a place in our future if we allow them in and we can bring them with us to play a different role from before. Death may end a life, but not a relationship. Our loved ones will live on in the hearts of everyone they touched. The Scottish poet, Thomas Campbell 1777- 1844, said it perfectly when he wrote, *'To live in the hearts of those we leave behind is not to die.'*

The Journey into Empowerment:

Remember death is not a thing that happens to life, it is a thing that happens within life. During our lives we are going to suffer tragedies, losses and setbacks. Try to remember that as human beings we have the inbuilt resources to overcome all obstacles that life will throw at us. This is a book to guide you to be the change in your life that you need, because the greatest support in your loss is going to be yourself. Yes this broken tear-filled shadow that was once a fully formed member of society is now stranded and shipwrecked on a desert island, broken and hopelessly waiting for someone to come and repair them. But what if that help doesn't come?

Tomorrow morning when you stare in the mirror take a deep look and say hello to your knight in shining armour, our Man Friday. And don't worry if this soggy eyed excuse for a human being staring back at you is not what you expected or wanted to see, angels come in many disguises. Say hello to your higher self. Yes this may be a time to lie low, shelter and self-soothe but I promise you, in time your grief will ease and the dark clouds that are engulfing your world will clear. No storm lasts forever and you may feel trapped in this prison by a cruel jailer. When we are faced with extreme tragedy in our lives which we never imagined or previously experienced, we will often shut down our lives in an effort to avoid annihilation.

This is a natural protective reaction. We shut out all our exposure to external stimulus and pain in order to survive. Unfortunately by doing this we also shut out all the joy in our lives that we had both previously and presently; everything that we took so much for granted, prior to our loss. We have left ourselves with little choice. We either decide that life is no longer worth living or else we rise wounded and broken and decide that we are no longer going to dwell on the painful part of our journey. We must begin to make a new narrative from the ashes to create and find new imaginative ways to make at least part of our lives more bearable.

While enduring this pain and loneliness we will find meaningful ways to rebuild our lives. You will discover that the lock on the prison door is on the inside and the cruel jailer is your alter ego. Leaving the prison has risks because you are deciding to face your grief head on and the comfort of knowing that as long as you remain there then no one can hurt you further or get to you. Unfortunately staying in your prison means a life with no joy or hope for a better tomorrow. We can only change when we change our internal reality. We can do this when we change our subconscious thoughts. When we experience a significant loss our lives are forever changed. For some the passing of time will bring some measure of relief, but for others it can be the beginning of a lifetime of struggle. People will think they know you. They think they know how you will handle grief but the truth is no one knows, not even you. They are not there when you are alone with your grief, when you are lying in bed or trying to eat and all you want to do is cry or scream. They have no idea of the sadness and anger you are dealing with whilst projecting the façade that you are coping well.

The Higher Self:

The higher self is a term normally associated with multiple belief systems. For the purpose of this book I use it to describe our eternal conscious and our association with our infinite intelligence. This state, I believe, allows us access to our infinite internal reality and can connect us with a higher power and allow access to the best version of ourselves by providing inner wisdom. This philosophy is the basis of the twelve-step programme used in addiction recovery and countless self-help programmes. It is often referred to in the bible and is often the basis of our prayers. Proverbs 17.22: '*A joyful heart is good medicine, but a crushed heart spirit dries up the bones.*'

We Become what we Think About:

Earl Nightingale was an author and speaker on the subject of human character and development during the 1930s. He was commissioned by Dale Carnegie who amassed countless millions during his lifetime and you can still see his philanthropy in his funding of libraries and concert halls in America and the UK.

Despite his enormous success he was held back by fears and doubts of insecurity. His books such as *'Think and Grow Rich; the Essence of Success,'* and *'The Strangest Secret,'* along with his lectures, are widely available on the internet.

Unresolved Grief:

Imagine living with a constant scream inside your head. The scream is your own and no one else hears it. Trauma is not what happens to us but what happens inside of us. We disconnect in order to protect ourselves. These can be events that happened at any age and lie dormant. They can surface unannounced at any point and can cause long-lasting harm often triggered by bereavement but not necessarily so.

These emotions can include feeling under threat, abandonment issues, feeling unsafe, feeling ashamed and powerless as well as being frustrated that you are unable to identify the source of these emotions. Everyone has a different reaction to trauma, so you could be living what you would describe as a normal existence until a triggering event happens and you find your life becoming unmanageable. What's worse is the inability to describe this anxiety and not have words to explain how you feel even to yourself or others.

Unresolved grief is much more common than we might realise. We may have gone through the pain of loss and never really asked the question, *'Did I grieve or did I push my grief well out of my way to avoid the pain of loss?'* Low self-esteem, high levels of anxiety, the ability to be easily irritated and avoiding getting too close to people are just some of the symptoms of not dealing with your grief. We can be very creative at burying our feelings and concealing our thoughts and memories. Hiding them in a place well out of the reach of our consciousness only for these to be awakened by a bereavement that, in normal circumstances, should not leave us feeling so devastated. Time with suffering and unresolved grief is not a healer.

You may manage fairly well on a day-to-day basis but something unrelated may trigger your subconscious and leave you in a state of unknowing sadness. Sometimes self-examination of your thoughts can be enough, but more often you will need the help and support of a bereavement counsellor or trusted friend who knows you and can be trusted to share your feelings with.

Find a person who will not judge and will be sympathetic to your feelings. There are no time-limitations on unresolved grief so please don't think, 'That was decades or years ago, how can I be so upset after all this time.'

This is a very common misconception. It may feel embarrassing and risky to open up to a stranger or talk to a friend in ways you never have done before, but it is required for you to move forward or else it will remain unresolved, only to pop its ugly head up again further down the line.

You may suffer from unresolved grief if you have the following symptoms.

1. Feeling unattached and finding it difficult to feel connected to people other than on the surface. Treating everyone with suspicion.

2. Always needing to feel safe, either in your home or in the company of a small number of family or friends. Being afraid to experience new opportunities and often avoiding and fearing meeting new people.

3. Over emphasis in needing the approval of others, always needing to feel valued and involved.

4. Not feeling secure in your identity. Always craving reassurance and direction.

5. A feeling of self-loathing and/or imposter syndrome and not being good enough. Feelings that, if people really knew the real me they would dislike and not love me.

6. Easy triggered by suppressed memories, for example a song, smell or familiar feeling pushing you into depression or sadness for no apparent reason. Bouts of uncontrollable rage without serious provocation. Someone innocently says something and you feel a sense of uncontrollable rage and defensive stance, quickly giving way to feelings of embarrassment for your overreaction.

Everyone at some time will suffer some or all of the above but if these feelings are impeding your general happiness and well-being then maybe you should consider how you might best begin to tackle these symptoms. All of the above symptoms do not make you a bad person. It's just that you may be suffering some unresolved trauma and it's only your body's reaction to experiences buried deep into your subconscious.

If by reading these symptoms you see yourself or indeed feel even more confused, can I suggest you try self-hypnosis or self-examination. Begin by finding a quiet place where you will not be disturbed and imagine you are in a special cinema, the film is in black and white and you are the star of the screen. Start the film with recalling your earliest memories and when you get to a place where you begin to feel frightened or stressed, simply pause the film and project your present day self climbing into the screen and tell your younger self that you are from the future and have survived.

Give the young person a hug and return to your seat again to continue. When another scene makes you feel afraid simply repeat, stop the film and reassure the younger you that you are from the future and you have survived this event. Keep doing this for as long as necessary and as often as you wish. It will do wonders for your self-awareness and self-esteem. What you are doing is a form of self-hypnosis and is totally safe and self-affirming. You can do it as little or as often as you wish and you will be amazed how much better you will feel in a very shot length of time.

No one knows how they will react, either in the short or the long term, to personal loss. Our first reaction is to try to soothe ourselves in order to compensate for the feelings of loss and desolation. Sometimes we may turn to drugs, alcohol, smoking, gambling and any other deviation to avoid the pain of loss. At the outset I defend your right to live your life in any way you choose. It is not for me or anyone to know what is best for you.

However it's important to know that you may be susceptible to forming habits to avoid the pain of grieving that in the long term may not serve your higher purpose. It is important to examine your use of these types of distractions. If you are using things such as drugs and alcohol in a damaging way it might be worth taking a step back. If we develop a habit to ease our pain and find ourselves moving from temporary relief to excesses we will find ourselves on the road to dependency. We instead need to consider how we might redirect our lives in a more constructive way. If we find we are doing something to numb our pain then we are in danger of becoming a slave to our habits that won't serve us well in the long term. If you see yourself overindulging, just check with yourself, am I allowing or using this habit to avoid my pain? If the answer is yes then the enjoyment gives way to the necessity to soothe, and will have the opposite effect.

We can only really affect positive change when we decide to change our internal reality and we can change our reality when we allow our subconscious thoughts to change our thinking. Our subconscious thoughts are responsible for most of our habitual thinking. For example, if we want to learn something new then we are always using our conscious thoughts to teach ourselves. These thoughts are slow and deliberate until our subconscious mind accepts these as part of our natural thought process. This happens when the critical gatekeeper opens for these thoughts and allows them to become subconscious thoughts.

An example would be when learning to drive. New drivers will fumble with the clutch, brake and accelerator until through continuous repetition the manoeuvre becomes automatic. Once the subconscious accepts our continuous habits it becomes very difficult to undo, but not impossible. Just because you think your habit is embedded in your subconscious does not mean that you are unable to make effective changes if you so desire. Rewriting your neural pathways takes repetition, time and effort, but can be achieved.

Try by talking about how you feel to someone you can trust and/or feel a connection with. Perhaps consider making a journal of how you are coping both in the past and how you would like to feel in the future. Learn to be open and honest with yourself and others.

Make yourself a promise from this day on, 'I will never criticize my thoughts again.' As the saying goes, it takes guts to leave the ruts and the first step is the longest on your journey. Never think it has been too long and no one will understand. I have had experience of clients who have had bereavements dating back many decades. Grief and loss is no respecter of time. The best time to seek help is right now. No one is going to judge you and you don't need to have some story mentally prepared. I remember a client starting our first session with the words *'I haven't got a foggy why I am here and don't know what to say.'* My response was, *'You're in good company because that makes two of us.'* We both smiled and off we went into many weeks of long enjoyable and revealing conversations.

No two people will experience loss in the same way. When we love hard, we have to realise that we are going to grieve just as hard. The solid rock that you once stood upon has broken away and you are clinging on to your meaning structure while your world spins around you. You are holding on to memories of unplanned endings and countless challenges unfulfilled. In our brokenness we may never realise that we will be able to rebuild, renew or accept the inevitable. We can only do this by grieving in the moment.

Don't try to grieve about the past or the future, instead allow yourself to grieve in the moment because in the moment you will cope. It has been my experience that the more you hold onto what's been hurting and destroying you, the more painful it will be for you to detach and heal from that trauma. Learning to let go and move on to a place of acceptance isn't easy but necessary.

"Grief is dying within me. A great emptiness, a frightening void."
(Basil Hume)

When people say *'sorry for your loss,'* it may sound hollow and trite but try and think what are they saying sorry for? They are sorry that your world has literally fallen apart at the seams, plunging you emotionally into a hypnotic nightmare that you somehow know you will never really fully wake up from. What they are really sorry for is that your world will never be the same again. You have been condemned to a lifetime of *'what ifs?'* and *'shoulda, woulda coulda,'* or thinking nothing will ever be the same again. When you read these words please know that at a soul level, I am reaching out to you in understanding and doing my best to reassure you in some small way the unimaginable pain that you are experiencing at this time.

What you are thinking presently makes perfect sense to me. The good news is that there is life after loss, after failure, after heartbreak and rejections. My promise to you is that you can, despite everything that has happened, that YOU have the ability to, and will enjoy peace of mind again. The past, even-though it remains large and daunting, is exactly that, your past.

You can start a new chapter in your journey that you might never have imagined or possibly ever wanted. Your current chapter of your life is not the whole story about you and it is definitely not the final chapter. There is always a possibility for a new beginning. The heartbreak will morph into a new heartbeat. Just remember you are going to be OK.

In grief we are going to suffer and sometimes we are forced to make a choice. We can either suppress our grief in the hope of being accepted or deal with the pain of our grief and face not being accepted. When you learn to love yourself enough and understand your needs you will begin to move away from those who refuse to travel with you on your journey. Rather than always insisting on making the right decisions, make your decisions right.

We only have one life and we have no real way of knowing our decisions are always the right ones. Sometimes our decisions work out exactly as we had anticipated, other times we have no idea of the fallout. We are not blessed with the gift of hindsight, at best we are all guessing and no one has all the answers. We are all going to lose in life, it's just the way the world is. If you wait until the right time to stop grieving it will never come. You must learn skills to support yourself, learning to walk again through life with its uncertainty is difficult but not impossible. We need to rid ourselves of the fantasies waiting for better times to come.

If we love much we will grieve much. Our grief will never completely go away. Some days our grief may be like a large stone in our pocket and other times as small as a grain of sand but it will always be there.

'Remember me' by Margaret Mead:

To the living I am gone
To the sorrowful I will never return
To the angry I was cheated
But to the happy I am at peace
And to the faithful I never left

I cannot speak but I can listen
I cannot be seen but I can be heard
So as you stand upon a shore, gazing at a beautiful sea,
As you look upon a flower, and admire its simplicity
Remember me

Remember me in your heartbreak
Your thoughts and your memories
Of the times we loved, the times we cried.
The times we fought, the times we laughed
For if you always think of me, I will never be gone.

An edited extract from Fahrenheit by Ray Bradbury:

Everyone leaves something when they die. A child, a book, a painting or a house. A wall built, a pair of shoes made or a garden planted. Something you had touched in some way, so your soul has somewhere to go when you die, and when people look at that tree, or that flower that you planted, you're there.

It does not matter what you do, as long as you change something from the way it was before you touched it, into something that's like you after you've taken your hands away.

The difference between someone who just cuts the lawn and a real gardener is in the touching. The lawn cutter might just as well not have been there at all, but the gardener will be there a lifetime.

Chapter Three
The First Phase of Grief.

The first phase of grief is disbelief and your inability to comprehend the enormity of the situation. We can often dive into denial and behave in a stoic and admirable fashion. This will last for as long as it lasts, but it will end. At the outset it may surprise and comfort those near to you that you display amazing acceptance, calmness, strength and constraint while everyone around you is losing their minds. This will help you deal with a myriad of details that need your attention immediately so the numbness is a necessary aspect of the early days of grieving.

- You may remember little of this period of shock after a death. The sorrow and pain are masked for us to allow us to cope, but the rage of anger and bewilderment will make us scrutinize the events and we may lash out at those near and dear to us at a later stage.

- You may be angry for any number of reasons that may seem irrational to those around you.

- You may take great offence to someone you would have expected to support you or attend the funeral, or even call but didn't.

- You may have issues with the medical professionals, funeral service, undertaker or family and friends.

Try not to be too hard on yourself, remember there is no wrong or right way to grieve and others understand that. Whatever way it passes it is what it is and try consoling yourself in the knowledge that in that moment you did the best you could with the information you had. One of few positives is you never have to explain or apologise. Hindsight is a wonderful thing and we all can use the words *'if only.'* In the passing of time when the shock will subside and we learn to face the finality and reality of our loss we will come to understand this.

It is natural to weep and become preoccupied with the loss. We delve into our memories including the last encounter as well as our unfulfilled dreams or ambitions. Often unresolved quarrels or an inability to make even the most basic decisions can wreak havoc with our emotions. Your relationship and connection to the deceased will be a major part of how you will grieve. This may depend on any number of types of relationships. You wouldn't expect someone who lost a distant relative or casual friend to grieve the same as a parent, partner, child, brother, sister, or neighbour. Whatever the relationship, it can have a devastating effect for any number of reasons. Your relationship with the deceased may have been hidden for personal reasons to either party leaving you to deal with a bigger loss than others will be aware of.

What were the wishes of the person who has died, if any? Some people will leave details and have strong opinions about what sort of funeral they would have liked. Carrying out someone's final wishes can be an important way of showing respect and be your final act of kindness. Deciding the type of funeral or service can be a difficult event even when the deceased has made their wishes known in advance.

Problems can and will arrive when no such discussions are had or if you are not the next of kin. Well-meaning family and friends will have opinions and things to say. Remember these decisions can't be revoked. If you are the next of kin and find yourself in disagreement with those who were in a relationship with the deceased try to do what is best for you and any others that you feel could benefit from your decisions at the risk of causing some pushback from others.

This could be decisions about viewing the remains or having children involved in the funeral procession for example, maybe seeing or touching the body is not something you would see as an option. Maybe you will have to have a funeral with no body available. Maybe you can't deal with being the centre of attention or squirm at the thought of being hugged by strangers. Maybe you have issues with too much emotion and causing hysteria. Try not to worry about what others think.

One of the certainties in life is that we will at some stage experience loss. This may be sudden or unexpected. It may be peaceful or tragic, planned or unplanned. Well-meaning family and friends will offer what they think is good advice and support and, not wanting to seem ungrateful, we kindly nod and agree with whoever is offering their words of wisdom and comfort.

How often have you watched on TV or listened on the radio to a reporter talking about a tragedy and saying the family need closure. It has been my experience that you never get closure. Because this would imply that you will forget, and no one alive wants to be forgotten in death. Our loved ones were too important in life to be forgotten. The good news is that we can, in time, come to terms with loss and bereavement and rebuild our lives in countless meaningful ways.One of the main aims of this book is to teach you to follow your heart and not the crowd, to take you from fear to freedom.

Resting in Peace (RIP - while your life is in turmoil):

The writer Virginia Ironside is an author, journalist and a problem editor at the Woman on Sunday newspaper and writes that before her father passed away suddenly she thought she knew about bereavement and would send out countless amounts of good advice on how we should cope and look after ourselves during bereavement. When her father died suddenly she found the rage of bereavement to be chaotic and messy. She describes how her father's passing had completely shattered her world leaving her in utter turmoil, with grief being only one small part of her rage, loathing and hatred for life. From all this she found a renewed interest in religion and the afterlife.

Grief, I have learned, is all the love you want to give but cannot. All of that unsent love gathers up in the corner of your thoughts; the lump in your throat and that hollow part of your chest.

'Grief is just love with no place to go.'

(Jamie Anderson)

'The most beautiful people we have known are those who have known defeat, known suffering, known struggle and have found their way out of the depths. These persons have an appreciation of and a sensitivity to the life that fills them with compassion, gentleness and a deep loving concern. Beautiful people do not just happen.'

(Elisabeth Kubler-Ross)

Chapter Four
The Moment.

The moment you are bereaved everything changes. It's like falling through a trap door with no return and only through your grief you will get to know your grief. Your first reaction is to close your eyes and try to go back to how it used to be but you know in your heart you can't. The reality is things will never be the same again. Your world that was, is different now. You are different now. You may crumble and fall to pieces but part of you remains in the here and now, however reluctantly, because we as humans have evolved to survive these experiences. We know there is a future waiting for us and we have no choice, we have to claim it. We may struggle with countless moments and go through dark days and sleepless nights but there is a light at the end of the tunnel.

Your life begins now. No matter what life experience you have had, you will enter this new journey with no clue of how to make sense of your loss, leaving you with no alternative but try to make sense of some very challenging and/or frightening emotions at a very deep non-verbal level. You know that you must wrestle with this angel of death because you can't afford the luxury of losing your mind and composure when others are doing just that.

The most challenging and scary part about bereavement is that we must change. Up until the moment we are bereaved we think that we can somehow stay the same. From personal experience I have learned that you never really feel old as long as one of your parents is alive and when you are orphaned, even as an adult, you experience grief differently. No two people will ever experience loss in the same way, all experiences will be different so please be careful when talking to someone and be careful about saying *'I know exactly how you feel.'* The bereavement may be tragic, sudden or the end to a long illness. You may feel totally unprepared to accept the reality of the situation. The passing after a prolonged illness may bring temporary relief only to turn into feelings of guilt for allowing yourself a few moments of self-care. When someone decides to let go to end their life all of the above feelings are multiplied and come to the fore.

Often as a temporary method and in order to cope we can freeze our feelings. For example, how often have you sympathised with someone who is bereaved and they have said I am just numb? I have learned that this is a natural and important way to cope. We can often berate ourselves later for being so removed from the realisation by zoning out from the whole ritual leaving nothing but a blur, but we must not be so hard on ourselves. These feelings are just part of normal grief and please remember in grief you never get it wrong so in order to heal you must never allow any self-criticism. Remember in your journey through grief to follow your heart and not what society would expect.

You will never really recover from your experience of loss. Words like closure and recovery are used to rebuild oneself but there is no way back, only ahead, and you may well say, *'how do you expect me to move on?'* How can anyone go back to the person they used to be? The answer is you won't, because your loved one has crossed this divide and left you with their unfulfilled hopes, dreams and a lifetime of what could haves and what should haves. Healing has more to do with trying to find a sense of balance and making decisions about making the abnormal at least a bit more bearable for the time being. If your bereavement has left you with dependents then you won't have the luxury of self-care because your attention, energy and focus will be on the welfare and care of others.

While there is no end or final destination for how your grieving will ease, in time you will find a place for yourself and the love you had inside will find a home again. It will come with living alongside your pain and loneliness, and overcoming the fear that having a few good hours or days will not mean you are somehow cheating your bereavement detail.

Your challenge is to try to make sense of what is, what was lost, and what's left. You will, in time, learn that the broken heart you have experienced is open again and will let in light for a new reality. The memory of your loved one will move into this light and attach itself to your heart. This coming together will emerge from a state of brokenness to a place of replanting and new growth. The best you can hope for at the outset is a sense of peacefulness. You will eventually have opportunities to experience your life in different ways without any sense of destination, just a lived experience. You will also discover imaginative ways to learn to own your grief. If your loss is recent then this may not be the right time to wonder about healing but maybe, just maybe, you might consider what healing might be like when it should come. Grief does not recognise time or place and does not set any rules. Your only guide is your gut feelings.

My Nan's Coat:

'My nan died yesterday. When someone suffers from a terminal illness you think you will know what to expect when they eventually pass away. You like to imagine that you will be somewhat emotionally equipped for it. I was under this impression too, and for the most part I was right. I was composed when I received the message that she had passed and when I arrived at the house and saw her afterwards, and when the doctor came to verify her death. I was composed when I kissed her forehead for the last time and watched the undertaker take her away. I held it together for almost the entire day.

It was only when we were getting ready to leave her house that the silliest thing got to me. I caught sight of her coat hanging off the banister. It was the most profoundly forlorn thing I'd ever seen. It had not been moved since she had last placed it there. When she had placed it there it was the last time she ever left her house, on Christmas day last year. It was hung there when she arrived home like it would be on any other day, only it didn't know that this would be the last time it would ever be worn again.

There was something so hauntingly sad about seeing it hang there in its normal place like it was waiting to be picked up and worn again. It wasn't until this moment that I realised she was really gone. It dawned on me that gone isn't some throwaway term or vast black hole by which you can define the absence like a vacant armchair, or the slippers by her bed, or a redundant coat hanging off the end of the stairs.

Gone is the half-finished scarf in my nan's knitting bag and the packet of jelly babies in her treat cupboard with only half of the contents left. Gone is dreadfully harsh. We tell ourselves that the people we love will be around forever, until one day they aren't any more. I know you are missing them now, that it feels like a deep ache from a part of yourself you did not know existed until the day you lost them. Just remember they will live on within you and not just in your heart, but in the way you infuse your care and kindness into everything you do.'

(Anonymous)

Twenty Things to Remember when Rejection Hurts:
(by Angel Chernoff)

Be OK with walking away. Rejection teaches you how to reject what's not for you. As you look back on your life, you will realize that many of the times you thought you were being rejected by someone or, from something you wanted, you were in fact being redirected to someone or something you needed. Seeing this when you're in the midst of feeling rejected, however, is quite tough. I know because I've been there.

As soon as someone critiques, criticizes, and pushes you away - as soon as you are rejected - you find yourself thinking, 'well, that proves once again that I'm not worthy.' What you need to realize is the other person or situation is not worthy of you and your particular journey.

Rejection is a necessary medicine. It teaches you how to reject relationships and opportunities that aren't going to work, so that you can find the right ones that will. It doesn't mean you aren't good enough, it just means someone else failed to notice what you have to offer, which means you now have more time to improve and explore your options.

Will you be bitter for a moment? Absolutely. Hurt? Of course – you're human. There isn't a soul on this planet that doesn't feel a small fraction of their heartbreak at the realization of rejection. For a short time afterwards, you will ask yourself every question you can think of.

- What did I do wrong?
- Why didn't they care about me?
- How come?

But then you have to let your emotions fuel you in a positive way! This is the important part. Let your feelings of rejection drive you, and inspire you on to a powerful opening to the next chapter of your story.

Honestly, if you constantly feel like someone is not treating you with respect, check your price tag. Perhaps you've subconsciously marked yourself down. Because it's you who tell others what you're worth by showing them what you are willing to accept for your time and attention. So get off the clearance rack. And I mean right NOW! If you don't value and respect yourself wholeheartedly, no one else will either. I know it's hard to accept but think about it. All too often we let the rejection of our past dictate every move we make thereafter. We literally do not know ourselves to be any better than what some intolerant person or shallow circumstance one told us was true.

It's time to realize this and squash the subconscious idea that you don't deserve any better. It's time to remind yourself that...

1. The person you liked, loved or respected in the past who treated you like dirt again and again, has nothing intellectually or spiritually to offer you in the present moment but headaches and heartache.

2. One of the most rewarding and important moments in life is when you finally find the courage to let go of what you can't change, like someone else's behaviour or decisions.

3. Life and God both have greater plans for you that don't involve crying at night or believing that you're broken.

4. The harsh truth is, sometimes you have to get knocked down lower than you have ever been to stand up taller and emotionally stronger than you ever were before.

5. It's not the end of the world – and yet it is the end of the world - and yet rejection can make the loss of someone or something you weren't even that crazy about feel gut wrenching and world-ending.

6. Sometimes people don't notice the things we do for them until we stop doing them. And sometimes the more chances you

give, the more respect you lose. Enough is enough. Never let a person get comfortable with disrespecting you. You deserve better. You deserve to be with someone who makes you smile, someone who doesn't take you for granted, someone who won't leave you hanging.

7. Some chapters in our lives have to close without closure. There's no point in losing yourself by trying to fix what's meant to stay broken.

8. Take a deep breath. Inner peace begins the moment you decide to not let another person or event control your emotions.

9. You really can't take things other people say about you too personally. What they think and say is a reflection of them, not of you.

10. Those with the strength to succeed in the long run are the ones who build themselves up with the bricks others have thrown at them.

11. Let your scars remind you that the damage someone has inflicted on you has left you stronger, smarter, and more resilient.

12. When you lose someone or something, don't think of it as a loss, but as a gift that lightens your load so that you can better travel the path meant for you.

13. You will never miss out of what is meant for you, even if it has to come to you in a roundabout way. Stay focused. Be positive.

14. Rejections and naysayers aren't that important in the grand scheme of things; so don't let them conquer your mind. Step

forward! Seriously, most of us do not understand how much potential we have – we limit our aspirations to the level someone else told us was possible.

15. Too many people overvalue what they are not and undervalue what they are. Don't be one of them. Ultimately, you are who you are when nobody's watching. Know this! And dare to be yourself, however awkward, different or odd.

16. Comparing yourself with others, or other people's perceptions, only undermines your worth, your education and your own inner wisdom. No one can handle your present situation better than you.

17. The more we fill our lives with genuine passion and purpose, the less time and energy we waste looking for approval from everyone else.

18. You can use your struggles, frustrations and rejections to motivate you rather that annoy you. You are in control of the way you look at life.

19. Sometimes transitions in life mean something even better is coming your way, so embrace them and don't be afraid to let go.

20. Right now is the beginning. The possibilities ahead are endless. Be strong to let go, wise enough to move forward, diligent enough to work hard, and patient enough to wait for what you deserve.

Afterthoughts - All details aside, you don't need anyone's consent, affection or approval in order to be good enough in this world. When someone rejects or abandons or judges you, it isn't actually about you. It's about them and their own insecurities, limitations and needs. So you don't have to internalize any of it! Your worth isn't contingent on other people's acceptance of you. In your grief you must be allowed to be yourself. You must be allowed to be your own voice, your own thoughts and feelings. You must be allowed to assert your needs. You must be allowed to hold on to the truth that who you are is more than enough. And have the courage to let go of anyone in your life who endlessly makes you feel otherwise. If someone is trying to control you it can often be in the form of care. It can look like care but it may be actually control. Just check that this care is actually going to better you or is it something that is going to better them. Always allow yourself to question absolutely everything and everyone. You can only heal when you know that you are not at the mercy of others no matter how well intentioned their motives are.

'The dead are not distant or absent. They are alongside us. When we lose someone to death, we lose their physical image and presence. They slip out of visible form into invisible presence. This alteration of form is the reason we cannot see the dead. But because we cannot see them does not mean that they are not there. Transfigured into eternal form, the dead cannot reverse the journey and even for one second re-enter their old form to linger with us a while. Though they cannot reappear, they continue to be near us and part of the healing of grief is the refinement of our hearts whereby we come to sense their loving nearness. When we ourselves enter the eternal world and come to see our lives on earth in full view, we may be surprised at the immense assistance and support with which our departed loved ones have accompanied every moment of our lives, in their new transfigured presence their compassion, understanding and love take on a divine depth, enabling them to become secret angles guiding and sheltering the unfolding of our destiny.'

(John Donohue, extract from his book
Beauty: The Invisible Embrace)

Chapter Five
The Art of Forgiveness.

All of us at some time in our lives have been hurt and wounded by the actions, words or deeds of another. If we focus on these words and deeds it becomes a habit and habits are difficult to break. Forgiveness does not mean absolving others of their responsibility for what happened. It means letting go of the hurt, anger and pain that was inflicted on you and putting the hurt back to the person who hurt you. For some of you reading this I hear you shouting that you have no idea what this person did to me. How do you expect me to just walk away and forget after all the pain? Holding a grudge is the same as carrying an anchor around continuously loaded with bitterness.

If you only knew the damage we inflict on our well-being when we hold on to a grudge. It is a poison inside us that festers with no relief. When you decide to forgive you immediately realise that you never have to think of them in this way again and allow a great weight to be lifted off your shoulders. One of the greatest gifts we can give to ourselves is the gift of self-forgiveness. When you no longer decide to be your own worst enemy you become open to a life of inner peace and joy the like of which you never thought possible. When you apply forgiveness miracles will happen. We can never grow spiritually when holding grudges.

Letting go of these thoughts requires great courage because we imagine our revenge and the sweet anticipation of getting even. If someone were to offer you something and you refused to accept their offer then it belongs to the one who offered it in the first place. It was never yours to begin with. So from now on simply refuse to accept anyone's opinion or criticism. No matter what someone has done to you, and I know this is very difficult to accept, but for your own healing you must learn to let go. If you don't let go then your life will be dogged with bitterness and anger and will colour everything else in your world. You should not forgive as a gift to the person who has wronged you, instead do it as a gift to yourself.

I must stress there is a great difference between forgiveness and forgetting. You can forgive without forgetting what happened. You may never forget, but you can choose forgiveness. In an ideal world the person will come to you and seek forgiveness but in reality this very seldom happens. That is their choice and they must live with the consequences. You only need to control your own behaviour not anyone else's. From now on only deal with your healing and not the hurt. Wayne Dyer puts it very well in one of his many books. He says that *'holding a grudge is like taking poison and hoping the other person dies.'* He asks the reader to consider that maybe the journey through major hurt isn't so much about becoming anything, maybe it's about unbecoming everything that isn't really you, so you can be where you were meant to be in the first place.

Sometimes you have to walk away and if you do, do it with a clear heart and mind. If you owe me, don't worry about it. If you wronged me, it's all good and lesson learned. If you are angry with me, you win, I have let it go. If we are not speaking, it's alright, I truly wish you well. If you feel I wronged you, I apologise, it wasn't intentional. I set you free and in doing so I release all the negativity that soured our friendship. I wish you and I every happiness from now on.

Always remember, forgiving someone is for your benefit, so don't block your blessings. Always remember that this too will pass. Whatever the experience we live through right now, be it good or bad, painful or pleasurable, remember these words: *'This too will pass.* 'These words will help focus your thoughts to appreciate the moment. Remember life is right now! It's not later! It's not when you retire, it's not when your lover gets here. It's not when you move into the new house. It's not when you get the better job. Your life is right now because it's not going to get any better than right now…

The Gift of Forgiveness:
(Edith Eger from her bestselling book, *'The Choice'*)

Dr Edith Eger is a therapist, author, and teacher. Her books are recorded on the New York bestselling list. She has lived through unthinkable trauma. She knows that the greatest prison we create is not by society or governments but by the mind. She does not hate because if she did, she would still be a prisoner of the past.

'So many people struggle to find joy in their lives because they are stuck in the past, stuck in loops of self-doubt, trauma, and criticism. They confuse forgiving with forgetting the past or they think forgiveness is something we do for others, absolving them of the hurt they caused us. As a survivor of Auschwitz, I suffered deep depression in my adulthood created by my childhood trauma. My sister and I were the sole survivors of my family from the horror of the concentration camp. It took me many years to free myself from my mental prison, long after the war. At the same time, I did not have anyone to teach me how to do it. I had to learn the hard way. Fortunately, forgiveness is not hard to learn and practice, but so few people know how to do it properly.

Forgiveness is the most powerful gift we can give ourselves RIGHT NOW to lift the heavy weight off from our lives. What would your life be like if you felt more energetic? More present? What could you achieve if you freed yourself from the burden of past regrets, trauma, and anxiety?

It all starts with the remarkable and often misunderstood power of forgiveness. We owe it to ourselves. We owe it to our loved ones. To be present. To be the best version of ourselves. To boldly face the challenges of our past and lovingly embrace the joy in life before it passes us by.

Learning the gift of forgiveness is what freed me from my mental prison. I owe my life to it. I deeply hope you learn to experience it in your life as well and make today a beautiful start.'

Boundaries Around Grief - Message to Friends:

Please forgive me but while I love having you in my life and appreciate your continuous support please remember you are not responsible for managing my grief. It's not your job to walk on egg shells or to avoid my triggers or keep the peace at all costs. I must learn that it's my responsibility to deal with my grief and begin to heal my own wounds and engage in self-care so that I can regain and maintain healthy boundaries.

In order to heal I must detox myself from my fear, anger and resentment. I am aware that every emotion in my body is dealing with the now along with the residue of the past, and whether I like it or not, whatever the present moment brings I must accept it. But I know I have bills to pay tomorrow and I am still going to grow old and die just like everyone else. Please allow me total surrender to suffer, to shuffle back and forward with my emotions.

Whether you pushed me or pulled me, drained me or fuelled me, loved me or left me, you are my reason for growth, so thank you. From now on I won't face reality. I will create my own reality.

Death and what Next?

When you finally give up the hope that the past can be any different, then you are ready to read this book. Yes I am aware I am repeating myself but I just need you to really understand this concept.

1. My mind still talks to you and my heart still looks for you, but my soul knows you are at peace.

2. Forgive anyone who has caused you pain. Keep in mind that forgiveness is not for others, it's for you. Being able to forgive is a vital part of your healing journey. This does not mean having people in your life who don't share or respect you. It's about you moving on in your life.

You do not get to choose the events that come your way or the sorrows that interrupt your life. They will likely be a surprise to you, catching you off guard and unprepared. You may hold your head in your hands and lament your weak condition and wonder what you ought to do, but to suffer is a part of life. However to come through this suffering and still keep your composure, your faith, and your smile, that is remarkable. Pain will change you more profoundly than success or good fortune.

'Suffering shapes your perception of life, your values, your priorities, and your goals and dreams.'

(Pastor David Crosby).

Heartbeat:

If we can self-destruct then we can heal. If we are defeated, then we can rise up again. If we can grow weary, then we can grow mighty. If we can be drenched in light and still feel the darkness then we can be drenched in darkness and still feel the light. What

I am trying to say is that in every good soul, I can still hear your heartbeat, and where there is a heartbeat, there is a way back home.

Ten painful truths worth remembering:

1. The average human life is relativity short.

2. You can only live the life you create for yourself.

3. Being busy does not mean being productive.

4. Some kind of failure always comes before success.

5. Thinking and doing are two very different things.

6. You don't have to wait for an apology to forgive.

7. Some people are simply the wrong match for you.

8. It's not other people's job to love you, it's yours.

9. What you own is not who you are.

10. Everything changes every second.

Grief:

'The reality is you will grieve forever. You can never fully get over the loss of a loved one, but you will learn to live with it. You will heal and you will re-build yourself around the loss you have suffered. You will be whole again but you will never be the same. Nor would you want to.'

(Healgrief.org)

'To honour you I get up every day, take a breath, and start another day without you in it. To honour you I laugh and love with those who knew your name, and smile and the ways your eyes twinkled with mischief and secret knowledge. To honour you, I take the time to appreciate everyone. I listen to music I know you would have liked and sing out to you. So now I live for us both, so all I do is honour you.'

(Unknown)

When I Go:

'When I go, don't learn to live without me. Just learn to live with my love in a different way. And if you need to see me, close your eyes, or look in your shadow when the sun shines, I am there. Sit with me in the quiet and you will not leave. There is no leaving when a soul is blended with another. When I leave, don't learn to live without me, just learn to look for me in the moments and I will be there, I promise.'

(Penny Ashworth)

Forgiveness:

Anyone can hold a grudge, but it takes a person with character to forgive. By learning to forgive you release yourself from carrying a painful burden. But deciding to forgive does not mean what happened was OK, and it doesn't mean that the person should still be welcome in your life. It just means that you have made peace with the pain and are ready to let go.

Forgiveness allows healing and provides the choice to take responsibility of how you are now going to view yourself from now on. It takes great courage to begin to dislodge long held beliefs entrenched in your memory that are no longer serving you while keeping you stuck in a just world mindset.

You may want to forgive your parents:

- For raising you through their own unresolved trauma. Just try to see that they did the best they could with the limitations life put in their way.

- For not being able to understand you, because they did not have the capacity to.

- For not being able to teach you certain skills because no one taught them.

- Our parents may have been unemotional and unable to relate to us because their parents were unemotional also. We can't fix our lives with the same mindset that created our thoughts, we must try to develop a new way to deal with our situations.

- For doing the best they could with what they knew and had.

- For following cultural norms that they were surrounded with.

- For raising you through their own cultural struggles, worries, pain and fears.

When you forgive someone, it doesn't mean that you accept their behaviour or trust them, it means you forgive them for you, so you can let go and move on with your life. Forgiveness is not something we do for other people. It is something we do for ourselves so we can move on.

When people say I'm OK, what it really means is:

- I don't know how to communicate my feelings
- I don't trust that you can handle what I feel
- I don't want to burden you

- I'm not ready to talk
- I'm trying to be strong
- I'm avoiding what I feel
- If I talk about how I feel I fear I will crumble
- I've been conditioned to pretend I'm OK even when my world is falling apart
- I don't want to appear weak in your eyes

Supportive statements when someone needs to talk:

- I am happy to listen if you want to talk.
- That sounds very difficult.
- What is the best way I can support you right now.
- I am sorry you are going through this.
- I believe you and what you are saying makes absolute sense to me.
- What I admire about you in this moment is ...
- You have every right to be upset.
- It's not your fault.
- Thank you for trusting me with this. It must be very difficult to talk about this.
- Anything you confide to me will never change my opinion of you.

You might never know the true impact you have on those around you. You will never know how much someone needed that smile you gave them. You will never know how much your kindness turned around someone's life. You will never know how much someone needed that long hug or deep talk, so don't wait to be kind.

Don't wait for someone else to be kind first. Don't wait for better circumstances or for someone else to change. Just be kind because you never know how much someone might really need your presence at that moment of grief.

Mistakes are the Portal of Discovery:

There is a difference between regrets and mistakes. In recent years I have learned to slowly allow myself to make mistakes and live with my regrets and allow self-compassion. We all make mistakes that we really regret. I have learned that it's better to be gentle with ourselves and allow our mistakes to help us grow. Sometimes in our lives our decisions can lead us to places and experiences we never intended for ourselves and others. I have learned to be compassionate with myself and found it very healing.

Self-forgiveness is our gift, not only for ourselves but others as well. Sometimes in life our decisions will have the desired effect and other times we can never really understand how our decisions can impact others. This is part of being human and I believe we are all guessing our way through life despite what our ego and the status of those we look up to would have us believe. No one is certain of anything, and we are at best guessing.

I happen to believe that we are spiritual beings having a human experience and our journey through life is to experience this contrast. We can often default to our childhood conditioning, when we make mistakes, we are punished, and punishment deserves retribution. We have to learn to put down the sword and let things go.

Boundaries:

It's not my job to:
- Heal others.
- Please others at my expense.
- Make it work if the effort isn't mutual.
- Continuously compromise.
- Tiptoe around others.
- Anticipate your needs.

It is my job to:

- Heal myself.
- Listen to my needs and my desires.
- Respect myself and my time.
- Be my true authentic self.
- Set healthy boundaries that protect my energy.
- Recognise and leave when I am not being valued.
- Say no when it's not in alignment.
- Be mindful with your yes.

Please don't ever get tired of being a good person with a good heart. I know it's horrible being taken advantage of, and driving you to be less caring than your nature. It is courageous people like that who give the world hope. With the risk of rejection please still offer your support and allow others to accept or reject it, and remember it is not for your benefit anyway. No matter how you try you are going to meet negative people who have a problem for every solution.

It is not your job to teach anybody anything, life has a way of teaching us all we need to know. Even with your expertise about a subject, allow others to disagree no matter how right you are, it only adds more stress and push backs. Make yourself a promise from now on to take time for yourself, to live the life that you came here to live, and to live it without ignoring your responsibility as a parent, spouse, or employee. Life is like an echo, what you send out comes back. What you sow, you reap. What you give, you get back. What you see in others already exists in you.

Take them With You:

If someone you love did not make it on the trip of life you can take it for them or with them. If someone you love did not witness that milestone you can show them any time you like.

If someone you love did not get to do their living, you can finish those dreams on their behalf. The beautiful thing about love you see, is that death need not stop life.

'If you carry someone in your heart you can take them with you, anywhere you like.'

(Donna Ashworth)

Talk about the deceased not because you are stuck or haven't moved on, but to celebrate their memory. Talk about them because we are theirs and they are ours and no passage of time will ever change that.

The Five types of Courage:

1. Physical courage... to keep going.

2. Social courage… to be yourself unapologetically.

3. Moral courage… doing the right thing when it is uncomfortable

4. Emotional courage… feeling all your emotions, positive and negative, without guilt or attachment.

5. Spiritual courage… living with purpose and meaning through a centred approach towards all life and oneself (wishing you well today).

From now on work on things that people can't take away from you.
- Your Character.
- Your mindset.
- Your integrity.
- Your authenticity.

Grief can be a juggling act. You are trying to heal, while trying to grieve, while trying to live, while trying to dream, while trying to smile, while trying to give love, while trying to be love to those around you. Grief, I've learned, is really just love. Grief is just love with nowhere to go. People assume grief is a sad experience following the death of someone you love. And you have to push through it getting to the other side.

It's been my experience there is no other side and pushing through is pointless. There is however absorption leading to adjustment and finally a level of acceptance. You will never complete this mourning, but you will learn ways to endure. In time you will find a new way of seeing a new definition of self. In the passing of time you will look back on this phase of your life no longer condemning, blaming, or guilt tripping yourself, allowing you to feel appreciation of the experience knowing we can only experience life with contrast.

You can't really begin to appreciate life until it has knocked you down a few times. You can't really begin to appreciate love until your heart has been well and truly broken. And you can't appreciate happiness until you have known sadness. Once you climb this mountain the view is breathtaking.

'Grief will come in waves of sadness, try to imagine that you are riding the waves rather than being drowned by them. Don't deny or push the grief away, instead find a quiet place to reflect. Think of ways you might begin to distract from your grieving thoughts and feelings. Think of past hobbies, interesting books or anything that will absorb your thoughts.'

(John Wilson
Supporting People through Loss and Grief)

'The reality is you will grieve forever. You will not get over the loss of a loved one. You will learn to live with it. You will heal and

you will rebuild yourself around the loss you have suffered. You will be whole again but you will never be the same, nor would you want to be.'

(Elisabeth Kubler-Ross)

'Write it on your heart that every day is the best day of the year. He is rich who owns the day and no one owns the day who allows it to be inundated with fret and anxiety. Finish it every day and be done with it. You have done what you could. Some blunders no doubt crept in but forget them as soon as you can, tomorrow is a new day. Begin it with a promise to yourself that your spirit will not allow it cumbered with your old nonsense. This new day is too dear, with its hopes and invitations to waste on the yesterdays.'

(Ralph Waldo Emerson)

I Choose to Live:

*'I choose to live by choice,
not by chance to make changes, not excuses.
To be motivated not manipulated,
to be useful not used, to excel, not to compete.
I choose self-esteem, not self-pity.
I choose to listen to my inner voice,
and not the random opinion of others…
I choose to be me.'*

(Miranda Marriott)

Walk Away:

*'Walk away from people who put you down,
Walk away from fights that will never be resolved.
Walk away from trying to please people
who will never see your worth.
The more you walk away from things that poison your soul,
the healthier you will be.'*

(Paulo Coelho)

80

Humour:

Some of us grew up learning to use humour to prevent tension and taking on blame we didn't deserve. This taught us to become scapegoats and people pleasers later in life to keep the peace, so it's such a big deal when we finally decide to be serious about standing up for ourselves and finding our voice to say, *'Enough!'*

Finding Balance:

The most important part of healing is finding your balance again, if only for a short time. We must look for balance in our being and our doing. We always have to manage our day to night existence. There is a time too for action and a time for rest. Always allow yourself to find your balance. We can kid ourselves that we are too busy to think and avoid dealing with our pain, making it almost impossible to move forward.

Grief and loss can and will leave us feeling overwhelmed and unable to progress. Often people will say I don't know what to do. I would suggest don't panic, just sit with your pain knowing it's alright not to know, and promise yourself that when you do know you will make good choices for yourself. Not knowing what to do is because you don't have sufficient information, and you promise yourself that when you have the right information you will make only good decisions for yourself on your own terms.

Always remember that you no longer have to prove anything to anyone. You no longer need or seek others approval and you don't need to explain even when you are accused of saying something that isn't true. Allow no one to rob you of your peace of mind. When you suffer great loss one of the few consolations is that you know that nothing as hard as this is ever going to hurt you as much again. Fate has done its worst and played its trump card and you are very much still in the game.

Chapter Six
Living One Day at a Time.

Having spent the better part of my life trying to either relive the past or experience the future before it arrives, I have come to the belief that in between these two extremes is where you will find peace. Life is right now, it is not later. It's not when I retire, it's not when my lover gets here. It's not when I move into my new home or when you get that dream job. Your life is only right now! It will always be right now. You might as well begin to enjoy life because it's never going to get better than the present. Try and be mindful of your friends and surroundings and appreciate them all in the now. For my journey it was about letting go the need for certainty. When you let go the need for certainty and use you innermost thoughts as a guide doors will open beyond your most fertile imagination. Give up the need to look for outside events for your happiness. So many of us rely on our external events to influence our behaviour.

Clarity and Connection:

Be prepared to meet a new version of yourself every time you shed another layer of old trauma, conditioning or hurt as you let go your perspective and your interests will shift. Transformation is natural as you travel the road to greater self-awareness happiness and peace. There will come a time in life when you walk away from all the drama and people who create it.

Surround yourself with people who create happiness not drama. Surround yourself with people who make you laugh, forget the bad, and focus on the good. Love the people who treat you right.

Pray for the ones who don't. Life is too short to be anything but happy. Falling down is a part of life, getting back up is living.

The Reality of Loss: (Grief is very Difficult to Describe):

I often use the analogy of the game of snakes and ladders. Some days you can throw a six on the dice and be on top of the world and in another instant find yourself at the bottom of the slippery snake having to start all over again. Other times grief can be like one of those Russian dolls. You open it up and deal with all your emotions only to find another roadblock with similar issues and you must begin the whole process again.

Unfortunately unlike the Russian dolls, these issues do not reduce in size. Grief will take you places you never knew existed; a place where we don't have words or meaningful ways to explain. There is nothing in this book, or any book I have read, that can provide an explanation or give clarity on this. Grief is a knowing feeling and despite the best intentions of family and friends you are very much on your own journey.

The only thing I can offer to you at this moment is that your feelings, emotions and actions make perfect sense to me. In this part of Ireland we pride ourselves as being good storytellers and you will find yourself telling the same story over and over again only to discover, no matter how much you change the details and events, you can never have a different ending.

At times you may find yourself talking to complete strangers who will look at you, trying to disguise with their facial expression the truth that they are relieved that they are on the listening side of this bereavement. Sometimes others will encourage you to stop thinking about it and try to take your mind off your grief. Trying to force yourself to not think about something has a nasty way of bringing on even more misery. There are non-grievers who despite having your best intentions at heart are unaware of the pain of loss and missing that smoulders inside. This slow-burning fire can't be extinguished, nor can it be consumed like a normal fire. Only time and gentle soothing can bring moments of temporary relief and respite from this relentless nightmare. On a personal note from my own journey, I remember meeting people in supermarkets, how they would look me in the eye and say, *'but how are you really doing?'* I felt they were intruding, looking for intimate details I didn't want to share. Learning to shop was one of the first tasks I had to inherit, and while my wife loved the whole shopping experience I found I had to shop in a different town fearing I would literally fall apart. Looking at items that we would no longer need would compound my grief.

When is the Right Time?

Letting go... I have often listened to clients asking me when is the right time to start dismantling the life they have lost, fearing that they are now somehow co-conspirators in accepting the fact that their loved one is not coming home again. These are very difficult and personal decisions and only the bereaved can decide when. This decision should be respected for whatever they decide or not decide to do. I tell clients they will never get this wrong. In life we have to make decisions and sometimes these decisions work out well whilst other times they are not what you would have liked or expected.

When people say they don't know what to do I would reply, don't do anything because when the time is right you will be able to make those decisions that serve your best interests. Everything we do in life will have consequences and when you have to make serious decisions let your heart as well as your head guide you in these matters. Just remember when you love much, you will grieve much.

What Other People Think of You:

We spend so much of our time trying to get approval and seeking the good opinion of others. In reality what others think of us is really none of their or our business. This is probably a difficult concept to accept when you have lived all your life looking for validation and approval from significant others. When you get to this position in life that you are indifferent to the good opinions of anyone it's very freeing.

We discover sometimes even late in life, that we have given so much of our personal power and self away at the whim of others. Now is the time to take that back. We spend all our lives and exhaust our energy trying to keep up some unrealistic ego-driven outward version of ourselves because we have this notion that somehow at the back of our minds we feel unworthy of acceptance. This is learned behaviour but can be reverted with careful self-examination. You can reboot and install a new version of the real you.

When you watch young children at play, just observe how they unconsciously interact with each other playing games in their full flight of enjoyment. Then well-meaning adults take these children and mould them into conforming well-disciplined and self-conscious youths - a one size fits all person, fit for serving society. Some young children will be fortunate enough to have parents to defend their young meaning structure.

Sadly many will be victims of the well-meaning adults who are passing on their unknowingly damaged core beliefs. Then for good measure add a dose of religion, and what you have is a good law and rule abiding citizen unable to say, feel or act in ways that they originally felt. They will, if not checked, in turn pass this on from generation to generation.

Sometimes you may think it is important what others think of you, and so you work to extract their approval, however there is really little you can do to keep their approval coming, for it was never about you, but about them.

12 Steps to Guide you to Find Happiness
by Robert L Stevenson:

Known for such works as *'Treasure Island'* and *'Dr Jekyll and Mr Hyde,'* Stevenson also wrote the *'12 Rules to Live By.'* His positivity would not be out of place in today's self-help industry and has stood the test of time.

1. Make your mind up to be happy by finding pleasure in simple things.

2. Make the best of your circumstances. No one has everything and everyone has something of sorrow intermingled with gladness of life. The trick is to make laughter outweigh the tears.

3. Don't take yourself too seriously. Don't think that somehow you should be protected from misfortune that befalls other people.

4. You can't please everybody. Don't let criticism worry you.

5. Don't let your neighbour set your standards, be yourself.

6. Do the things you enjoy doing, but stay out of debt.

7. Never borrow trouble. Imaginary things are harder to bear than real ones.

8. Since hate possesses the soul do not cherish jealously, enmity or grudges and avoid people that make you unhappy.

9. Have many interests, if you can't travel then try and read about new places.

10. Don't hold postmortems. Don't spend your time brooding over sorrows or mistakes. Don't be someone who never gets over things.

11. Do what you can for those less fortunate than yourself.

12. Keep busy at something. A busy person has never time to be unhappy.

'If you want to be happy you have to let go of the part of you that wants to create melodrama. This is the part that thinks theirs is a reason not to be happy. You have to transcend the personal and as you do, you will naturally awaken to the higher aspects of your being. In the end enjoying life's experiences is the only rational thing to do.

You are sitting on a planet spinning around in the middle of absolutely nowhere. Go ahead, take a look at reality. You are floating in an empty space in a universe that goes on forever. If you have to be here then at least be happy and enjoy the experience. You're going to die anyway. Why shouldn't you be happy? You gain nothing by being bothered by life's events, it doesn't change the world, you just suffer. There's always going to be something that can bother you if you let it.'

(Michael Singer from 'The Untethered Soul')

Jordan Peterson, born 12th June 1962, is a Canadian author, psychologist, media commentator and Harvard lecturer and has in equal measure attracted support and criticism on gender identity.

His second book, *'12 Rules for Life,'* is a multimillion best seller and below is a very brief summery. He argues that there is a right and a wrong way to live your life.

- Rule 1 - Fix your posture. Others will treat you with more respect.

- Rule 2 - Take care of yourself, the way you would take care of someone else.

- Rule 3 - Surround yourself with people who want you to succeed.

- Rule 4 - Judge yourself by your own goals, not by others.

- Rule 5 - As a parent, train your children to follow the rules of society.

- Rule 6 - Before you blame anything else, think; have I done everything within my ability to solve the problem?

- Rule 7 - Do what is meaningful to you, and you will feel better about existing.

- Rule 8 - Act only in ways in line with your personal truth. Stop lying.

- Rule 9 - Listen to other people thoughtfully. You'll learn something and they'll trust you.

- Rule 10 - Define your problem specifically. It's easier to deal with.

- Rule 11 - Accept that inequality exists.

- Rule 12 - Life is tough. Take time to indulge in little bits of happiness.

Eckhart Tolle is a German-born spiritual teacher, author of the *'Power of Now'* and *'A New Earth.'* The following is a transcript adapted by the author on why there is only now.

When your mind is taking you to all sorts of unpleasant places, you can come back to knowing that we only have this moment. No one wants to manifest suffering deliberately but millions of people daily do exactly that.

We must learn that it is ourselves that manifest our own suffering. We think the blame for our suffering is always elsewhere and never in our mind. You can blame bereavement, God, Karma, fate, destiny, your parents or whatever else you choose that they are the cause of your suffering. We don't realise that it is our mind that is manifesting our thoughts. People who are not ready to hear that can get very angry. It is the unconscious mind that manifests this suffering. It's the narrative around the situation that makes you unhappy.

When you finally discover and realise that, it's the first stage of awakening. At this moment it's an amazing discovery that all your suffering is actually created by your mind. You come to the conclusion that you don't want to manifest negativity anymore and you now have opportunities to manifest something else. You can be open to making good decisions about your problems. Always remember when you feel tension arising it is caused by your thoughts at that moment. Instead, gently allow yourself to think positive thoughts and learn the secret of living in the moment.

This is the state where opportunities will form within to provide you with positive solutions never before considered. The secret to life is you have all the power. If you can change your mind you can change your life. You don't need any amount of money or education or connectedness. You just need to be in control of your mind remembering you have what it takes.

Relationships:

The relationship you have with yourself is the most complicated one you will ever have. You cannot ever walk away from yourself. You have to forgive every mistake. You have to live with your flaws. You must always look for ways to love yourself when we are absolutely disgusted by our own actions. The relationship you have with yourself is the most important one you have so learn to work on it daily. Learn to love yourself without condemnation because you are worth it.

Being Alone is the Capacity to Love:

It may look paradoxical to you but it is not. It is an existential truth that only those people who are capable of being alone are capable of love, of sharing, of going into the deepest core of another person without possessing the other and without reducing the other to a thing without becoming addicted to the other.

They allow the other absolute freedom, because they know if the other leaves they will be as happy as they are now. Their happiness cannot be taken away by the other. It is not given by the other.

'Love is not turning to a partner and depending on them to fix you and make you whole. You have to be whole entirely by yourself. Love is turning to a partner and asking them if they can sincerely stay by your side and support you while you figure out yourself, your life and your healing.'

(Meredith Marple).

Chapter Seven
Protecting Children from Grief:
Why Children are Unbeatable?

As adults we will always want to protect children from the pain and desolation of loss. Children are likely to notice when something is wrong and may feel fear and display signs of being under stress. Like adults grief can affect them in many different ways, and children would prefer to know what is happening. When they hear a person has died they may not react, or show little or no emotion leaving you thinking that they are not aware of the situation. This of courses depends on the age and stage of the child's development as well as whether or not they have siblings. Children may not always use words to express how they feel. Depending on the age of the child they may regress by using old comfort blankets or asking for their bottle and in some cases begin wetting the bed again. Older children may find it difficult to concentrate at school and fall behind in the classroom.

When I was growing up in the 1960's it was a different world than we know now. I have often heard, and to my regret would have said it myself at times, that the odd slap didn't do me any harm. It was only when I went into deep self-examination later in life that I realised that this was not a true or accurate assessment. So much so that when I hear this remark now I look at the person and try to see their hidden and often buried pain.

In those days the use of corporal punishment was widely accepted, but as we know now was, *'of its time.'* Parents, teachers and others in authority felt they had a legal and moral right to punish children, saying things like, *'this is for your own good,'* or *'spare the rod and spare the child,' 'don't let children rule the roost,'* or *'you're making a rod for your own back'* were common examples of the rationale used. It is an undisputed scientific fact that talking to children is good and violence is bad. It's that simple. Parents must practice non-violence, using words not blows. If you want your children to be good make them feel good. Young children need to learn how to recognise their own feelings including anger, frustration and sadness in a safe and non-threatening environment. Physical punishment makes the child angry instead of sorry. Physical punishment only stops the child from doing something right now, it does very little to change their behaviour.

I'm not saying let your children do as they please, in fact quite the opposite. Children need boundaries and must be encouraged to share with other children. They also need to take turns and be patient. Children need to be taught what is acceptable and not acceptable without the threat or use of violence.

Many clients I have worked with often much later in life, recall painful moments when a teacher or parent would lash out at them in anger making them feel humiliated and would have to endure their wrath. They would seldom see the connection to further life challenges when they would find themselves with similar feelings of helplessness and despair.

According to Dr Dorothy Rowe, children when abused will do either one of two things. They will blame the person abusing them or most likely, blame themselves thinking they were wicked and therefore deserved to be punished, and punishment means pain. To avoid pain people will close down into depression and anyone who has been depressed knows how awful it is. It's like a prison, you feel you are locked in a small room and while it is a form of protection and safety, it is also a place where you are alone and all light and happiness is taken away.

92

Children and Young People and their Understanding of Death:

(Amended from the Irish Childhood Network)

Children will feel similar emotions to adults when they lose a loved one, but they can't express it the same way. Instead, they may express themselves with outbursts of anger, excitement or sadness. Sometimes they might seem like they've accepted the death, but later become angry, distressed and upset. It's important they are given the time, space and the support they need to manage this. They may often repeatedly search for the deceased and imagine that the deceased person has returned. Children need to be allowed to jump in and out of emotions often crying uncontrollably in one moment and playing in the next.

They should be allowed to display temper tantrums and not be overly criticized for these outbursts as they are natural and often the only outlet for expressing grief. There will be changes in academic performance along with anxiety that someone else close to them will die. They may also cause trouble by taking unnecessary risks. They may display signs of bullying or being bullied. All of the above are no more than signs that they risk losing control and need to seek attention to help them work through their grief. Crying in front of your children can give them permission to show their feelings too. Using words like gone to sleep or gone away can lead to confusion and trigger thoughts that others they depend on will go away too.

The cause of death should be age appropriate and great care taken so as the child does not in any way blame themselves. Children may find drawing or making things useful in expressing their grief. Making a memory box with the children is a good way to allow the child to express their emotions. These can contain any item that is a positive reminder of the bond they had with the deceased. How children understand and react to grief depends on their age and stage of development. Grief is a heavy burden for a child to carry continually, so they need to put it down sometimes. Grief changes as children get older. As they grow and mature, their understanding of death increases, and they may need to revisit the loss again over the years. It can often be surprising for adults that children are talking or upset about loss that happened perhaps years earlier when the child was much younger. It is very natural for them to try to understand the loss when they have developed a better ability to do so.

Children's Understanding of Death:

- *0-2 years* - After a death in the family it is common for a baby or toddler to become withdrawn or display outbursts of loud crying and angry tears. Although infants do not understand death, they know when things have changed, and may react to a person's absence. This may show in clinginess and distress. Support them by maintaining the same routine and always try to make them secure.

- *2-5 years* - Children gradually learn that death is final and that all people will die at some time. This may lead to worry that others close to them will die also. It is good to let children talk about their fears. We can't promise children that no one will ever die, but we can help them to feel safe by telling them that they will always be looked after. More curious children in this age group often ask direct questions about what has happened to the body as they are trying to understand. They may try to blame themselves in some way for the death and can fantasise about information that has not been shared by significant others in their lives. Always encourage them to talk and encourage them to draw or write about their feelings and never criticise them for anything they may share.

- *8-12 years* - This age group will understand that death is irreversible and will be asking for a cause. This age group may express their grief by challenging behaviour and physical aches and pains. This can be found more often in the eldest children who may take on the role of a parent who has died by becoming the *'man' or 'woman'* of the house. They will need constant reassurance about the family home and financial income as well as the security of the family unit. They will be watching the surviving parent or guardian for cues on how they are coping and often can take on the same fears and anxieties.

Adolescence is always a difficult journey. Young adults struggle with their sense of identity and striving for independence and a bereavement will heighten their struggle with these issues. Adolescents will need clear and accurate information at the time of death. Try to include them in the rituals and treat them in a manner appropriate to their age. They may or may not want to take an active part in the funeral arrangements and may decide to mark the death in their own way. Family pressure can direct them not to show emotion at the funeral for fear it may adversely affect other family members. Respectful arrangements and allowances that suit the adolescence should be observed at the risk of upsetting older family members and always please respect their autonomy.

Often an adolescent will display withdrawal emotion and this is just a temporary display in order to make sense of what has happened and their lack of experience in dealing with death. Try to avoid argumentative behaviour. You can expect a drop in school grades, anger, sadness and withdrawal from social interaction.

- *15-18* - Mourning will be more adult in manner. Teenagers at this stage will often try to integrate their past relationship to the parent who has died, what the parent expected from them and may find ways to live up to those expectations. At this age they will understand the enduring consequences of the loss and be in a position to see the situation from another's perspective. At this age they would be engaging in planning their own future. They may try to exaggerate their maturity in order to mask their inability to cope. Watch out for use of drugs and/ or alcohol to help numb the pain. They may express blame at anyone they feel that might be responsible for the death, often becoming withdrawn and not wanting to become involved in any family or social activities. They may also want to protect the parent from their pain. Try to be patient and don't react to their responses to loss. Seek help if you suspect they are in denial that the death has occurred, are suffering prolonged depression or have suicidal thoughts or actions or displaying a tendency to self-harm.

Our children will deal with loss and bereavement in direct contrast with how the significant others in their lives can share the gift of their own happiness.

Dr Gabor Mate is an internationality renowned Hungarian author and speaker and is an expert on addiction, trauma and negative childhood experiences. He is one of the world's most revered thinkers on trauma and addiction. His writing helps us explore our loss and how our childhood trauma can cause us untold pain in our future. In his books *'When the Body Says No'* and the *'Hungry Ghost,'* he explains that unless we address these traumas we will always suffer and that unaddressed trauma is the major cause of chronic and life threatening illness if not addressed.

In his lectures and writing he explains how the body and mind are not separate and we don't need prescriptions to get fixed. Instead he suggests our personal transformation can bring forth the healing we need to get fixed. Prescriptions, he argues, come from the outside and transformation from the inside. His books are about detangling our life experiences. He states that addiction is often a compensation for what you lost in childhood. In his book *'When the Body Says No,'* he highlights how suppression of our needs in childhood can result in serious life-threatening illness later in life. Suppressing our needs undermines the immune system. Being a child of the Holocaust he experienced firsthand a lifelong perception of not being wanted. This resulted in becoming a workaholic doctor to ensure he always felt needed and all his life he had to justify his existence.

The Effect on a Family from the Loss of a Child:

Before you tell a grieving parent to be grateful for the children they have, think about which one of yours you could live without. Only those who suffer this loss can be a guide to the suffering. The death of a child will make some friends and family uncomfortable. Be prepared for those awkward moments, they will come. Those who are close to you may not always be around long after the funeral.

'The greatest loss anyone can face is the loss of a child. The experience doesn't change you, rather it completely demolishes you. The remaining days of your life are spent nursing the pain that you think will never go away.'

(Narvin Grewal)

When a child dies, and particularly for the parents, the effect on the family relationship is unimaginable. The parents may grieve in different ways. The father may be afraid to display his feelings as it may be interpreted as a sign of weakness and feels that he must be strong to support the mother and siblings.

The sheer pain of the mother's grief may leave her unable to support the father or her other children. There is a danger that the child who has passed will become the perfect child whom the siblings can never equal. This can cause the remaining children to overcompensate or try to match the standard left by the child who has passed. This can also continue to affect children born after the child who has died. There is also a danger that they could feel their birth is nothing more than a replacement rather than being wanted for who they actually are.

The loss will also greatly impact the grandparents as they struggle to support each other and the parents as well as the lost dreams and hopes for their future. Normal domestic rifts between family members after someone dies can be extremely difficult to manage and have the potential to end the relationship.

Chapter Eight
Positivity.

Do you pray? What is prayer?

'Prayer doesn't only happen when we kneel or put our hands together and focus and expect things to happen from God.
Thinking positive and wishing good for others is a prayer. When you hug a friend, that's a prayer. When you cook something to nourish your family and friends, that's a prayer. When we send off our near and dear ones and say drive safely, that's a prayer. When you are helping someone in need by giving time and energy, that's a prayer. Prayer is a vibration, a feeling, a thought. Prayer is the voice of love, friendship and genuine relationships. Prayer is an expression of our silent being. Keep praying always.'

(From the Mind Journal)

A Lifetime:
'It takes a lifetime to learn to live.
How to share and how to give.
How to face tragedy that comes your way.
How to find courage to live each new day.
How to smile when your heart is sore.
How to go on when you can take no more.
How to laugh when you want to cry.
How to be brave when you say goodbye.
How to love when your loss is great.
How to forgive when you want to hate.
How to be sure that God is really there.
How to find and seek him in prayer.'

(Norman Beattie)

Positivity:

Sometimes positivity may feel like you need to spend the rest of your days reading, repeating affirmations, praying, mediating or listening to brainwave entertainment. You could also experiment with hypnosis, subluminal messaging audio and whatever else is supposed to be holding you back from finding your true self. All of the above can support this process of self- empowerment but none of it is essential for you to ever feeling normal again. All of these applications are only roadmaps and directions, not the destination. How often have we learned, sometimes too late, that all we want and need is already within us?

Sometimes saying you are positive when you are not really can actually be potentially dangerous, especially if you use it as a smokescreen to avoid your true feelings. We can feel expected to project a positive image at all costs. A bit like if you fall out of an aeroplane and you're hurtling towards the ground, grabbing your handkerchief to use as a parachute, saying to your friends, *'I haven't hit the ground yet.'* Positivity, used as a smokescreen, can become very toxic. It is important to know that we are never perfect and are constantly a work in progress. Life will always present challenges and if we are willing to meet these challenges they will guide us to become a better version of ourselves. Accepting our human flaws and at the same time working out how we can overcome obstacles while still experiencing negative emotions and coping with day to day living can be extremely taxing but very rewarding.

Trying to remain positive when your life is crumbling around you as you struggle with feeling sad, scared or worried about how you are going to keep it together is all encompassing but what we should always focus on is that this too will pass. Storms, no matter how severe, never last, and the darkest part of the night is just before the dawn of a new day.

Try to focus on finding the best solution at the given moment rather than a final absolute solution. Try to avoid too much toxic positivity and instead try to be open to the possibility that we are only one decision away from creating a totally different life. I am aware that often life can ask you more than you are able to give. Often grief is about facing reality and how you face this reality will provide opportunities to create a new narrative for yourself. Often we can be only one decision away from a totally different life, even on the dark days. Loss can leave a heartache that no one can heal, but love will leave a memory that no one can steal. Courage is not the absence of fear but the ability to handle our fears in a more positive way.

For as long as we grow we will experience fear at some level. Often fear is nothing more than false evidence appearing real. Sometimes we don't love because we don't know love when we see it. Learning to recognise self-love is very subtle and not often visible to you. It only shows up when the event has passed. Self-compassion is always telling yourself that you are worth that compassion. The best way to deal with guilt is to make friends with it. When you try not to feel guilty you will end up feeling more guilty. The next time you have feelings of guilt just try to reframe these thoughts and be aware that guilt feelings are trying to make you feel bad and that bad people deserve to be punished.

Stop punishing yourself for events that were outside of your control. Just remember when as children, in order to survive we had to conform to our parents, teachers and anyone we considered important. Saying no in your childhood was never an option. As children we knew we needed significant others in our lives to survive. We knew at a very young age we had to depend on these people and often had to accept their definition of our inherent badness. To survive we believed this narrative and in so doing we believed we were somehow bad and deserved to be punished. These thoughts have often grown with us into our adult selves making us think at our core level we must be bad and no one should ever really know. When you find yourself upset in life about what anyone has said about you what you are actually thinking is that their opinion is more important than what you think of yourself.

What others think of you is none of your business. Other's opinions are just their opinion and that is all it is. When you give away your power and allow others to have control over you then they will always have it. We all need and crave approval. We love to hear nice things about ourselves. Just remember you don't require anyone's approval. When you crave external approval and you don't get it then you can feel upset and worthless. The strange thing about approval is that those who need it least always get the most and those who need it most never get enough. So if you want approval the first thing to do is stop needing it. Advance confidently following your own dreams and march to the sound of your own drum.

'A thought transfixed me.
For the first time I say the truth as it is set into song by so many poets, proclaimed as the final wisdom by so many thinkers.
The truth – that love is the ultimate and highest goal to which man can aspire. Then I grasped the meaning of the greatest secret that human poetry and human thought and belief have to import.
The Salvation of man is through love and in love.'

(Viktor Frankl)

Chapter Nine
Losing a Pet.

There is a cycle of love and death that shapes the lives of those who choose to travel in the company of animals. It is a journey unlike any other. To those who have never lived through its turnings or walked its rocky path, our willingness to give our heart with full knowledge that they will be broken seems incomprehensible. Only we know how small a price we pay for what we receive. Our grief, no matter how powerful it may be, is an insufficient measure of joy we have been given by our pets.

When your Dog Dies:
They tell you not to cry. It's just a dog, not a human being. Get over it, what will people think, so dry your tears. They tell you that your dog is no longer in pain and you should be glad of that. They might say that they wished that someone who loved them would take them to a place to be put to sleep when they come to the end of their useful life. They tell you that it's important not to let them suffer. They will say it was for their own good. They tell you that there is no more pain, but they don't know how many times you and your dog have looked into darkness alone when human friends are nowhere to be found.

They don't know how many times your dog was the only one who was by your side when others walked away. They don't know how much fear you have at night when you wake up with your grief. They don't know how many times your dog slept near you. They don't know how much you have changed since your dog became part of your life. They don't know how many times you hugged him when he was sick. They don't know how many times you acted like you didn't see her/him getting older and unable to express its puppy like traits. They don't know how many times you've talked to your dog, the only one who really hears you without judgement. They just don't know that it was just your dog who knew you were in pain. They don't know what it feels like to see your dog trying to say hello. They don't know when things went wrong the only one who didn't leave was your dog. They don't know that your dog trusts you every moment of its life, even if it's the last. They don't know how much your dog loved you and how it is enough for him to be happy just because you loved him. They don't know that crying for a dog is one of the most noble, significant true and warmest things you can do. They don't know when the last time you moved him how much pain he was in, making sure you didn't hurt him. They don't know what it felt like to pet their face in the last moments of their life. Not everyone gets to experience the purity of spirit and their ability to love unconditionally.

Our pets are much more aware of their inner being that we humans give them credit for. Our animals, simply by observing their human owners, offer no resistance and love unconditionally. They give nothing but pure positive energy showering us with love and special connection. Our pets do not hold grudges or re-play any past scenarios over again. Once an uncomfortable situation passes they let it go completely. If you find yourself wondering what to say to someone who has lost their pet, try to understand that it's not just the loss of the pet, it is the loss of connection. That connection can never be replaced by a new pet and allow the person time to grieve. You don't have to try to make someone feel better. Often just your presence is sufficient for them to understand that you understand their pain.

I asked a vet what was the most difficult part of his job and unsurprisingly he said putting a pet to sleep. His earnest request was that despite the anguish and pain, that the owners or at least someone very close to them be present. The act of euthanising is a very challenging procedure and when the pet knows it's surrounded by its human family this greatly reduces the distressing experience for your pet. It is the least we can do!

(Emanuele Spud Grandi [Adapted])

A Dog's last Will and Testament:

'To a poor and lonely stray,
I'd give my happy home,
my bowl and cosy bed,
soft pillow and all my toys,
the lap which loved so much,
the hand that stroked my fur,
and the sweet voice that spoke my name.
I'd will to the sad, scared shelter dog,
the place I had in my human's loving heart,
of which there seemed no bounds.
So when I die, please do not say,
I will never have another pet again,
for the loss and pain are more than I can stand.
Instead go find an unloved dog,
one whose life has held no joy or hope,
and give my place to him.
This is the only thing I can give.
The love I left behind.'

(Unknown)

Chapter Ten
Coping with Death.

Natasha Josefowitz is a lecturer at the Stein Institute in San Diego, California. She writes about death and grief. She says death can make us experts in things we never wanted to know. She states:

'It happened to me and I imagine it may have happened to you as well. We didn't want to go through the pain and devastation that may have brought us here, and yet here we are trying to rebuild our lives with more love than pain. Loosing someone close is a major wakeup call as we try to make sense of regret, remorse and a bit of shame which are a frequent comparison to grief.

Death teaches us that life is real. We learn much from the experience and love more intensely after experiencing profound loss. It is natural for us to feel sadness and grief after a loved one has died. Whether we like it or not, it changes us and we must transform. Grief, however much pain it brings, serves as a purpose to our healing and whether we like it or not, we become someone different. To survive we must be willing to live a life from a deeper place.

We can choose to learn from crisis. We are going to experience regrets when someone dies. Death can teach us that nothing is promised to us. It can open the door to live life more fully. Death will teach us that life is precious. When we come through the dark night of the soul you have an opportunity to find a new preceptive.

There is no cure or shortcut. Grieving is a journey and a process we all must take. Healing begins with first healing our thoughts.

When we change our thoughts we can change the way we experience life. Our thoughts will either move us towards healing or keep us stuck. In the early stages of grief you will shut down as if somehow your body has died too. While on the surface you may be able to walk around putting one foot in front of the other doing all the right things, your soul is still searching for your loved one in all your familiar places.

If you find yourself feeling this way and feel totally overwhelmed just remember that you must be gentle with yourself and I promise that it won't be long to allow the one you have lost find you. The veil between physical and non-physical is very thin. Allow your loved one to find you.'

Our First Steps Through Bereavement:

All of us at some time in our lives will face bereavement. Although loss and mourning are a normal universal part of being human, for those going through it, bereavement can be a sheer hell. Bereavement can be isolating and lonely. It will give rise to a bewildering cocktail of emotions and will affect you on countless levels including physical, psychological, social, spiritual and emotionally. The way we each experience bereavement will be different for all of us, it's uniquely personal. There is no blueprint for how to deal with it and there are no rules about what is appropriate or normal.

(Sue Mayfield - First Steps [Amended])

Every journey will be completely different. Despite this some experiences are similar. You will feel completely drained and unable or unwilling to function. You will be unable to eat or, like me, comfort-eat in an effort to cope and ward off feelings of hopelessness. Your decisions will be filled with remorse and consumed with guilt. You may feel exhausted and unable to get out of bed in the morning or you many have no emotions whatsoever. To family and friends and outsiders you will behave as normal while inside your private world you can be falling apart. You have little choice with this messy, ugly and debilitating condition and despite well-meaning family and friends this journey is one you must take alone.

If your bereavement was expected after a long illness you may also feel some relief that your loved one is no longer in pain and you can feel guilt for having this relief. If the passing was sudden then another range of emotions will hunt you down like a pack of wolves waiting for you to stumble. During the initial stage you may have surprised yourself and others on how well you were coping and how stoic you were when others were losing their minds. Then at a later stage when people complement you on how well you are doing whilst you're struggling internally.

Elisabeth Kubler-Ross (1926-2004) was a Swiss American psychiatrist and pioneer in near-death studies and author of the internationally bestselling book on death and dying. She writes about the stages of grief which I have elaborated on below:

- *Denial* - Denial can buy us time, so that when we can't fully register the total pain, shock and disbelief over our loss in one moment or day, or however long. So the pain is spread over time almost like a deferred payment on a credit card, and our inability to confront the loss adds interest to the loan. We often can convince ourselves that the loved one isn't dead and this can be a coping mechanism to help soften the blow and can bring temporary relief from complete devastation. You may say what's wrong with me because at this moment I don't feel anything. Feeling numb and frozen in the first few days is very normal and a common occurrence. Sometimes the shock is so overwhelming that our brains go into slow motion because often we have never had to face any situation similar and we struggle to make sense of what is happening.

- *Anger* - Anger is another natural reaction to loss, whether it's anger at the cause of death or the deceased for passing away. It could be focused on your God for letting this happen or somehow you blame yourself. How could a just God allow this tragedy to befall God-fearing people who never caused any harm to anyone? Anger is pain and allows the body to have permission to keep some distance from the loss and avoiding the reality of the separation. This can be a healthy expression to protect the bereaved and allow the reality to come in stages. You can be angry at almost anyone, for example the medical profession or maybe a person who didn't attend the funeral or any number of people. This anger can give you structure and divert you from a feeling of hopelessness and help you focus on the immediate tasks following the death. Don't dismiss anyone's anger after a loss and see it as a necessary part of grieving.

- *Bargaining* - When we are facing a bereavement or immediately after a loss we can begin to use statements focusing on regrets about what you did or didn't do before the person died. We will do anything to avoid the pain of loss. You may comfort your thoughts with words like, well they lived a full and happy life or they died doing what they loved. You may feel it's just a dream, one where you are going to wake up from and continue with normal activities. Praying for a miracle and defying the odds and having your hopes dashed.

- *Depression* - Depression or acute sadness is when the great loss begins to become a realization affecting your life in countless ways. The sadness feels like it will last forever, this depression can be immediate or years after the bereavement. Maybe you begin to withdraw from life and you wonder if it is really worth living any more. As part of our coping strategy we can maintain that our loved one is on an extended vacation and will return again. When we lose our partner we can also lose our circle of friends. We no longer want to be with people or visit places to avoid becoming upset. You can often feel like a spare wheel at social events and maybe rather than trying to hold on to these friendships, you could try to make some new friendships by joining new clubs or organisations. Don't give up entirely on your old friends as with time you can reintegrate but these new friendships can be very helpful in helping you move forward. During bouts of depression you may find yourself not knowing what to do and while this is very common and very frightening, I would suggest that just don't do anything and learn to trust your emotions. Say to yourself, 'when I do know then I will act but until that time comes around I won't be doing anything.'

- *Acceptance* - The final stage in the journey is not as some believe that life is going to be OK. Instead you understand that you are coming to a place where you can begin to accept that you can't change the past, and that realization will open a path for you to at least begin to heal. Then you are no longer a prisoner to your grief. You learn that you are the one keeping you in this prison and the key has always been on the inside. Acceptance is not a road to Damascus conversion, but a slow clearing of the fog allowing you to rebuild some parts of your life again. This requires great courage because often we become so accustomed to having bad days that often we can feel somehow guilty if we are not metaphorically dressed in black. You begin to understand that your loved one is never coming back and this realisation begins to take root in your new reality. Grief will come in stages and not in a straight line. It is my opinion that these stages only signpost us to how grief is supposed to feel. As you know there is much more that we can write about, we are only scratching the surface of the indescribable emotions that run amok around our emotions.

You will still have symptoms of grief and these steps are not linear. You may have different emotions every day and while you struggle to gain a grip on your emotions you can have a bad day any day. If you can imagine your grief is a ball inside a box, the ball is the size of a football. At the beginning of your journey, the ball takes up almost all the space in the box. Only by the passing of time and moving through the stages of grief outlined above the size of the ball will reduce leaving more space in your box for your life. On good days it may shrink to no bigger than a tennis ball and others it's only the size of a marble rolling around in your box. Then for no apparent reason something triggers your memory, it might only be something as harmless as a song or familiar smell, your ball inflates and you are right back into survival mode.

This is perfectly normal and with the passing of time will subside more quickly. I am reluctant to use phrases like 'letting go,' and 'moving on,' often at the impatience of friends and family. Always remember this is your journey and only you can decide how you are going to make sense of your loss. Some clients often fear moving on in fear of forgetting, or somehow disrespecting the memory of the deceased. It is my theory that those who love once can learn to love again.

Often during discussions with clients I would provide an extra chair and I would suggest to the client to imagine for a moment that it was them who had departed and their loved one was with me listening to the conversation about how awful life is. I would ask them, what would you be saying from your non-physical perspective? Everyone's answer was for the bereaved person to try and rebuild their life in ways that they would want them to. We would want this for our partners but are unable to have it for ourselves. *'I shouldn't laugh when I'm bereaved it isn't respectful.'* This is a very common complaint but laughter is deeply therapeutic and is nothing to be ashamed of. It helps us release tension and is an important part of our coping mechanism. Dark humour and the ability to laugh at life's absurdities are healthy and normal especially if the person who has died had a good sense of humour and enjoyed a good joke. An awareness that they would want you to be happy is very important and the fact that you are trying to enjoy life is a tribute to the person who you have lost. Learning to accept that now is the new normal for you and how often have I suggested to clients that it was never the deceased's job to make you happy. We have to find our own happiness and giving that responsibility to someone else, even though they are deceased, will lead to further depression. Happiness is an inside job and it falls within our gift to find happiness.

Author Napoleon Hill writes that, *'every adversity, every failure in life, carries with it the seed of an equal or greater benefit when we learn that loss and grief are part of life.'* Throughout our life, we will experience the death of loved ones, and grieve for them. It is painful and sad, working out what life looks like without the loved one can be difficult, and coping with the loss once it happens can be a struggle. Always reach out to friends or family, GP or bereavement counsellor, or someone from your faith community or a charity helpline. You do not have to deal with this alone.

Chapter Eleven
Dealing with People and Disputes.

If and when disputes and disagreements arrive, try to remember that everyone is dealing with their own grief and emotions, and they are not in a good head-space to make sensible decisions. Emotionally everyone is feeling very raw and maybe just a few hours or days apart may be necessary to let hearts and minds cool. If it is at all possible try to keep talking and communicating especially about how you feel. In the early days you might even carry on as if nothing has changed or you may even try to airbrush the memory of the deceased out of your conscious mind. At a later stage expect anger outbursts and a sense of losing control when everyone else seems to be holding it together. Try to remember all of these emotions are completely normal and never cast blame on anyone, especially yourself.

Funeral arrangements can be very taxing, especially if you are dealing with your partner's family. They will all have their own ideas about how they should be laid to rest. Just remember patience and understanding, it is very easy to say something in this period that can be taken out of context when everyone concerned is grieving. You may, as a couple or group, have very different views on moving on, for example in the case of a child with the bedroom being changed. A simple thing like removing posters from the wall or disposing or giving away special toys and clothes can cause a lot of turmoil. You may want to cherish these items while your partner may want to remove these triggers for their grief. Please just try to be compassionate with your feelings.

As a general guide I would not make any significant changes for at least one year and very slowly afterwards. How long will these feeling last? The truth is that healing is a very slow process and every day you may feel like the pain is just the same, and just as raw as it was when the day the deceased passed. What is happening is that your grief is like a huge screw turning very slowly and as far as you can see it's just turning randomly without direction or purpose. Please be assured like a screw-nail turning, there is a destination. You need to allow yourself time to process your feelings.

Don't compare your grief. Your grief is your experience and people will say they understand, but they cannot know the circumstances, even if their own grief was for the same relationship their grief experience will be totally different. Allow everyone to own their experience and it's not important who's more correct. Friends and family might think that your grief is out of proportion and will try to correct your view with what they think is a more realistic approach. They may even try to encourage you to have gratitude not knowing that pain and good things don't necessary cancel each other out. Just politely remind them that your grief belongs to you and with respect you get to decide about your decisions in your grief.

You don't need to deal with well-intentioned platitudes. People will want you to get over your loss. It makes more sense for people to get over their need for you to get over your loss because your loss makes them uncomfortable.

The Power of No:

How many times have you heard yourself saying yes to wrong people, overwhelming requests, bad relationships, time-consuming obligations, from well-meaning family and friends who find it easy to intrude into your world? How you wished you could summon the power to turn down requests, allowing others requesting the surrender of your joy in order to facilitate someone or something else. The word no is an incredibly painful word to say. How many times have you refused to say no with the end result causing much anguish, desperation, arguments and anxiety? You spend your time trying to second guess what will happen or how will someone react if you decide to say no.

You have the right to say no! You have the right to say no to anything that will directly hurt you! Direct no's are easy in comparison to the more loaded requests that leave you feeling guilty and selfish for having the courage to follow exactly how you feel. The good news is that sometimes saying no can lead to a better yes.

You have the right and are fully entitled to choose regardless of what society will try to impose upon you. You have the right to say no to anyone who tries to stifle your creative intentions. The consequences of saying yes to something you don't want will result in you hating what you are doing, anger and resentment of the person who asked you in the first place and you end up feeling hurt and disrespected by yourself and your inability to assert your true feelings. Sometimes people will demand answers immediately expecting that when they say *'jump'* for you to respond with *'how high?'*

Always remember you have the right to ask for time to consider, and allow yourself all the time you need to see how this request will affect you rather than rushing into a decision. Allow time. Weigh up the necessary ramifications before giving your decision. Learning to say no to physical, emotional or mental boundaries will come from a new understanding of your gut reaction to requests that intrude into your personal space.

If up until now you have allowed yourself to be manipulated, but you are beginning to protect yourself from being taken advantage of, this will result in others being surprised by your lack of concern for their intentions so expect to be called selfish and uncaring. Just remember how often in the past when you allowed yourself to be taken totally for granted and how you felt as a result.

You should not or could not be all giving without taking time and space to regroup your thoughts and feelings. By not respecting your time and space you will end up totally exhausted and unable to provide love and support, firstly to yourself and then to others as you so wish.

Always remember it's one thing to say no and it's very important to have the power to say no or yes if it's for the greater good of everyone and your decisions won't eat at you in the future. You can also still say yes but with your own caveats. For example, yes I can do that however at the minute I am dealing with X, Y & Z. Once I have completed these I will be able to look at your request.

It might be next week before I get the chance to do this. This means you have still tried to placate the requester but you have taken the pressure off yourself and the ball is in their court. If the timeframe for you to deal with it is too long the person may make other arrangements.

James & Claudia Altucher (Adapted from the *Power of No*)

Chapter Twelve
Death: the End or a new Beginning?

The final words of Steve Jobs:

The following is accredited to Steve Jobs by his sister Mona Simpson. (Steve Jobs passed away in 2011). These words have not been authenticated by the Apple Foundation but either way they make great sense.

'I reached the pinnacle of success in the business world. In others eyes my life is an epitome of success. However aside from work I have little joy. In the end wealth is only a fact of life that I am accustomed to. At this moment laying on my sick bed and recalling my whole life, I realize that all the recognition and wealth that I took so much pride in, have faded and become meaningless in the face of impending death. In the darkness, I look at the green lights from the life supporting machine and hear the humming mechanical sounds. I can feel the breath of God drawing closer.

Now I know that when we have accumulated sufficient wealth to last our lifetime, we should pursue other matters that are unrelated to wealth. It should be something more important. Perhaps relationships, perhaps art, perhaps a dream of your younger days – the pursuing of wealth will only turn a person into a twisted being just like me. God gave us the senses to let us feel love in everyone's heart, not the illusions brought about by wealth. The wealth I have won in my life I cannot bring with me. What I can bring is only the memories precipitated by love. That is the true riches which will follow you, accompany you, give you the strength and light to go on. Love can travel a thousand miles. Life has no limit. Go

117

where you want to go. Reach the height you want to reach. It is all in your heart and in your hand. What is the most expensive bed in the world? Sick bed... You can employ someone to drive the car for you. Material things lost can be found. But there is one thing that can never be found when it is lost...life:

When a person goes into the operation room, he will realize that there is one book that he has yet to finish reading - the book of healthy life. Whichever stage in life we are at right now, with time we will face the day when the curtain comes down. Treasure love from your family, love from your spouse, love from your friends. Treat yourself well and cherish others.'

(Steve Jobs)

His sister writes that at the end of his life he looked like someone whose luggage was already strapped onto his vehicle, who was already on the beginning of his journey, even as he was deeply sorry to be leaving. She writes, *'death did not happen to Steve Jobs, he achieved it.'*

Most of mankind throughout the millennia have chosen to accept that death is not the end, that we live on in some way or another. We hope that when our bodies can no longer function that there is something that awaits us at the end of our final journey, something that will humble us by its unearthly beauty and splendour that we will only be able to stammer, like Steve Jobs *'oh wow'* when we perceive it.

Death is our universal destiny. None of us will be spared its decree. We are not leaving this world alive. Yet its meaning remains cloaked in mystery. All of us will leave this earth without the certainty of our destination. Like Woody Allen, we claim we are not afraid of death but we just don't want to be there when it happens. We stubbornly persist in believing that we will somehow be the exception to the fate of humankind.

118

In some ways acknowledging mortality is liberation. Kris Allen's popular lyric offers the hope that you *'wish you could live life like you know you are dying.'* Every moment is more precious when you know it could be your last. Every experience is more intense when you're aware that it might never again be repeated. But the flip side is that fear of the unknown is debilitating and depressing. We have no idea what awaits us and there is still so much here we have left undone. We might never know what happens to our loved ones. We will never see our friends and family.

We wish we could know more about death and the closer we get to that meeting with the universal mystery, the more urgent our need to define it. Is death the end or a new beginning? So far science can't give us the answer but our tradition and religious outlook can try to shed light on the topic. The Christian faith teaches us that we retain awareness of our identity and we re-join our loved ones in time.

Elisabeth Kubler-Ross describes passing into death as breaking out of a cocoon and emerging as a butterfly and that our bodies during life represent physical limitations. Without them we are, for the first time, able to soar to heights previously unattainable.

From Grief to Healing:

Men and women grieve and heal very differently. Gender is a factor, life experiences, and the way we have been raised can alter how we grieve and make sense of our loss. Men tend to increase their activities after bereavement while women intend to decrease them. I repeat, there is no right or wrong way to grieve, but people do have expectations on how someone should grieve.

Never listen to anyone who tells you how it should be done. It is a very personal experience and men are more likely to go into denial.

Pre-grief people who were care givers at the end of the deceased's life need to be introduced to society very gently again. For them they had to change the relationship from a partner or close family member to a care giver and can lose so much of their individuality.

Often someone who is care giver for a long time can experience very mixed emotions which I have touched on before. While part of their new experience gives them the freedom to do things and go places that they only imagined, they are torn with guilt and confusion. Often when partners are widowed the relationship with the deceased family and friends change also. These changes can be subtle or sometimes quite profound. Everyone's grieving and some members of the family will want you to move on and be the same person you were before the loss, while others will want you to remain the same. However this is more often for their own benefit so as to fit their agenda.

In time you will have to learn to worry less about what other people think of you. From now on you will have to make what you think of yourself your new priority. In the past you may have spent your life trying to please others which never brought you the fulfilment you would have desired. In the past you may have had to put on hold your opportunities to find joy in living or exploring new experiences while never really feeling you deserved to be happy.

No matter what the past has brought into your world, from now on, make a promise that you will decide your own fate. This at first can be daunting because whilst it frees you from the bondage of other opinions it also removes passing on any blame about how you feel. It now must rest with you this new responsibility, freedom and power. Very soon you will experience alignment and discover stamina and clarity.

When you finally give up the hope that the past can be any different:

Some people survive and talk about it. Some will survive and go silent. Some people will survive and create. Everyone deals with unimaginable pain in their own way, and everyone is entitled to that, without judgement. So the next time you look at someone's life covetously remember, you may not want to endure what they are enduring right now.

In this moment whilst they sit so quietly before you looking like a calm ocean on a sunny day you have no idea of the internal turmoil they are experiencing. The ocean is vast and whilst somewhere the water is calm, in another place storms and hurricanes can be raging.

'Together we are all on a journey called life. We are a little broken and a little shattered inside. Each one of us is aspiring to make it to the end. None is deprived of pain here and we have all suffered in our own ways. I think our journey is all about healing ourselves and healing each other in our own special ways. Let's just help each other put all those pieces back together and make it to the end more beautifully.

Let us help each other survive.'

Ram Dass

Chapter Thirteen
Impossible Situations.

How often have we found ourselves in impossible situations with no obvious resolutions? Choices are something that only a few people can enjoy. We can lose our power and/or come to a wall in our lives. The causes are numerous. Our sense of place, financial circumstances, health, and any number of situations can render us to a prison of depression and insecurities. But there is a choice. We always have the power within us. Some of us may be locked in a physical prison where you would think choice is pointless. For most of us however our prison is in our mind. We can make very small changes and in doing so, provide ourselves with a little forward moving energy. It's the same as physical action. The tiniest action can spark us into a new motivation mindset.

The first step in any change in mindset is the most important. The other choice could be to do absolutely nothing, making no effort to change anything, saying this situation is impossible and I will never experience change. I cannot express how self-defeating that mindset is. There is always hope no matter how bleak things can become and it starts with the tiniest change of your thoughts. There are two things that create your world, the things you see in your head and the words you speak. No-one deserves to be in the situation you are in, not anyone and not you, but somewhere along the line, your life, your thoughts brought you to a situation that grew and grew until you were in this horrendous place. It's not your fault, you did not ask for this, but somehow this is what you got. Somehow life has got you here. By making the smallest change will help you feel you are beginning the first step on your journey to finding the key out of your prison. *'Baby steps,'* *'one day at a time,* 'these are standard sayings but they ring true. Begin by using mantras or prayers to the universe or your God. Try to meditate and centre yourself.

> *'I create freedom,*
> *I have freedom,*
> *I choose freedom.'*

Make this mantra a continuous supporting self-talk even in your darkest hour when sleep defies you or you think this is just impossible.

The Art of Being Yourself:

Dr Wayne Dyer would often refer to our life choices and how our thoughts can give us an opportunity to grow. He writes that we have two choices. You can begin with *'I don't like the person I have become.'* You try to fix your life and you can spend your whole existence trying to fix yourself. You will never get to a place where you are totally happy. You will live with the desire to always have more. When you set yourself a goal and you struggle to get there, you will discover that the goal was not enough so you will find another and start again. Or you can start saying to yourself, *'I am enough.'*

You are never going to get enough. You are and have everything you need. All you need to live a life feeling fully human and fully alive. We come into this world with nothing and we leave with nothing. All you have and require is your own uniqueness. If you really believe that your very presence on this planet is enough then you will begin to live a life of true contentment and joy. When you know you are enough you will soon discover you also have enough. Your circumstances have very little to do with your happiness, it's how you approach your circumstances that creates meaning in your life and makes all the difference.

Take what you are and accept it. Take your life in your hands, accept the person you are warts and all. Offer no attachment. Eighty percent of our clothes we never use. When your cup is full stop pouring. When you realise you have enough you are totally rich. Create balance in your life. Dyer always said, *'the sun never says no to the earth, you owe me!'* Practice having a state of contentment. His mantra was, change your thoughts and change your life. Learn to soften your thoughts. Ease away all rigid thoughts. The more flexible your thoughts the easier your life is. The more rules you make the more rule breakers you create. Have the courage to change your mind. Don't be afraid to say I don't know, not knowing is not a sign of weakness.

One of my all-time favourite authors and motivational speakers was the late Dr Wayne Dyer (10 May 1940 - 29 August 2015). He died of a heart attack in Maui, Hawaii. He spent the first ten years of his life in an orphanage when his father walked out on his family of three boys. He married three times and had eight children. He survived a cancer scare with no side effects and without any medical intervention. He had written over 45 books and was a much sought after public speaker. He didn't think Jesus was teaching Christianity and argued that Jesus was teaching kindness, love, concern and peace.

I have listed a few of his most popular quotes below but this is but a small sample of his work. He would always say that we are spiritual beings enjoying a human experience. He would often quote the Indian guru Nisargadatta Maharaj (1897-1981) who wrote that *'love says I am everything, wisdom says I am nothing.'*

- *'If you believe it will work out, you'll see opportunities. If you believe it won't you will see obstacles.'*

- *'If you change the way you look at things, the things you look at change.'*

- *'If prayer is you talking to God then intuition is God talking to you.'*

- *'You create your thoughts, your thoughts create your intentions, and intentions create your reality.'*

- *'For the spiritual being, intuition is far more than a hunch. It is viewed as guidance or as God talking, and this inner insight is never taken lightly or ignored.'*

- *'Your attitude is everything, so pick a good one.'*

- *'Every thought that you have impacts you. Shift from a thought that weakens you to one that strengthens you.'*

- *'If you don't make peace with your past it will keep showing up in your present.'*

- *'When you change your inner thoughts to the higher frequencies of love, harmony, kindness, peace and joy then you'll attract more of the same.'*

- *'Always be a student. Stay open and be willing to learn from everyone and anyone. Being a student means you have room for new input. When you are green you grow, when you are ripe you rot. By staying green you will avoid the curse of being an expert. When you know in your heart that every single person you encounter in your lifetime has something to teach you, you are able to utilize their offerings in profound ways.'*

- *'Everything we do is based on the choices we make. It's not your parents, your past relationships, your job, the economy, the weather, an argument or your age that is to blame. You and only you are responsible for every decision and choice we make.'*

- *'When we judge another, we do not define them, we define ourselves.'*

- *'If you continue to use the building bricks from the past you will end up building the same house.'*

Having the Courage to Change:

It takes courage to change because we don't like to admit to ourselves and others that maybe we got it wrong. If we begin to dismantle our thoughts like removing bricks from a Jenga game then we face the real possibility that our whole world may come crashing down. We face the chance of alienation and that can be scary. When we have faced enough negativity the time will come when we are ready for change. Finally when we are open to growth then we can make real changes.

We can begin with baby steps, nothing major, small changes. The first steps are the hardest but once we get the ball rolling it becomes easier. We can change because something has happened in our past that we no longer want to hold on to and at a gut level we know something has to change. Maybe you have tolerated enough, and you say to yourself screw this, what's the worst that can happen. How many things have we put up with in the name of keeping others humoured, at great personal cost? We can and should rewrite our own core believes. You don't need to justify to anyone why you want to change. The fact that you want to change is justification enough.

Personal growth is something we should all strive for in all walks of life and situations. You don't need anyone's permission or approval. If you give away your own happiness just to please someone else, then you are not truly living your live by your own standards and being honest with yourself. Who are you not being true to when you put your own thoughts to the side and allow others to dictate what we think.

Viktor Frankl was a Jewish/Austrian psychiatrist who survived Auschwitz. He used his experiences in the concentration camp and found a reason to continue living when the chances of survival were remote. The Gestapo had all the power and he was made feel less than human and degraded beyond comprehension. He knew that the only thing he could control and had complete power over was his thoughts.

He writes: *'Everything can be taken from a man but one thing; the last of the human freedoms – to choose one's attitude in any given set of circumstances, to choose one's own way. When we are no longer able to change a situation, we are challenged to change ourselves. The truth is if you are not being honest with yourself, who you are being true to? Learn to be a full version of yourself. Don't be afraid to be the full version of yourself, you are much too important to be a half version of yourself. In the words of Mai West, you only get one life and if you live it well then one is enough. Avoiding change because of pain does not have to be that way. The greatest pain is holding back, the true version of yourself is much more painful.'*

(Viktor Frankl)

Finding Meaning in Pain and Suffering:
(Howard C. Cutler from his book *'The Art of Happiness'*)

'Finding meaning in suffering is a powerful method of helping us cope even during the most trying times in our lives. But finding meaning in our suffering is not an easy task. Suffering often seems to occur at random, senselessly and indiscriminately, with no meaning at all, let alone a purposeful or positive meaning. And while we are in the midst of our pain and suffering, all our energy

127

is focused on getting away from it. During periods of acute crisis and tragedy it seems impossible to reflect on any possible meaning behind our suffering. At those times we wonder, *'Why me?'*

Fortunately, however, during times of comparative ease, periods before or after acute experiences of suffering, we can reflect on suffering, seeking to develop an understanding of its meaning. And the time and effort we spend searching for meaning in suffering will pay great rewards when bad things begin to strike.

We must begin our search for meaning when things are going well. A tree with strong roots can withstand the most violent storm, but the tree can't grow roots just as the storm appears on the horizon. So, where do we begin in our search for meaning in suffering? For many people, the search begins with their religious tradition. Although different religions may have different ways of understanding the meaning and purpose of human suffering, every world religion offers strategies for responding to suffering based on its underlying beliefs.

In the Buddhist and Hindu model for example suffering is the result of our own negative past actions and is seen as a catalyst for seeking spiritual liberation. In Judaeo-Christian tradition, the universe was created by a good and just God, and even-though his master plan may be mysterious and indecipherable at times, our faith and trust in his plan allows us to tolerate our suffering more easily, trusting as the Talmud says that:

'Everything God does, he does for the best. Life may still be painful, but like the pain a woman experiences at child birth, we trust that the pain will be outweighed by the ultimate good it produces. The challenge in these traditions lies in the fact that, unlike in childbirth, the ultimate good is often not revealed to us. Still those with a strong faith in God are sustained by a belief in God's ultimate purpose for our suffering.'

Love:

L is for listening to your heart.

O is for opening up to your emotions.

V is for being valued and valuing others.

E is for easing pain and healing.

I might Never Love Again:

When you survive loss everyone is quick to say how strong you are and how difficult it must be. But in reality we don't have a choice. Survival is not optional. You will cry into your pillow when watching TV and you will cry when praying for courage and strength. You know you don't have the luxury to put your life on hold. Even in your brokenness you are expected and needed to be there for others. You say I will cry tomorrow.

In the early stages of grief, when coming to terms with loss, we make statements to ourselves and anyone who will listen that we will never risk loving again. We believe we can never overcome this sorrow and vow to ourselves never to try again. We are sure we will never rise above the sorrow and promise never to embarrass ourselves by trying.

These self-fulfilling prophecies can be dangerous given the fact that our thoughts create our reality. I often encourage clients to delay in making any major decisions that can't be easily revoked. The old adage comes to mind, *'decide in haste and repent at leisure.'* Sometimes we try to avoid going into the state of grieving to avoid pain and possible rejections, and to avoid this we busy ourselves making changes that are not for our long term benefit.

I reiterate, clients often say, '*I don't know what to do.*' My reply is always to say, '*if you don't know what to do then don't do anything,*' because at this time you are not in possession of all the facts so wait for as long as it takes. You will know when you can make good and all necessary decisions again. Grief is no respecter of time, so take as long as you need to make good choices for yourself.

So often you will get pressure from family and friends to stop dithering and make changes that will ease their worry over you, but they don't realise this is making the situation worse. Their intentions may be good but the outcome is far from it. By moving on we imagine that we are somehow disrespecting the memory of the deceased and how special, how loved, and irreplaceable in our lives he or she was. Of course the deceased was unique and special but this denial of self can be a misguided way to express love and respect. Who in their passing would condemn their partner to a life of loneliness and remorse? Making plans and being open to the possibility of living and loving again should be your memorial to the memory of the loved one you have lost.

We often tell ourselves that true love only comes once in a lifetime. We are in danger of placing our loved ones on a pedestal and promoting them to sainthood. I've always said that those who love once can and should love again. While it's right to turn from unpleasant memories it can be self-deluding and add stress to your coming to terms with your grief. These thoughts can lead you to a place that's not real and idealization can prevent you from creating new relationships.

We are in danger of denying ourselves the prospect of making new, deep and special friendships. Being open to the possibility is often enough, you don't have to do anything just be open and learn to trust your emotions. This allows us to care about ourselves and enables us to set new boundaries while encouraging us to have our feelings respected and free from guilt. Sometimes healing can be slow and we can grow impatient, we must learn that there are many steps along the highway from sorrow to serenity.

We must be gentle with the different stages of emotion and the times of unbearable pain and disinterest in life. You must find a way to a new acceptance of the continuing challenges of life. Through my own journey I have learned that things don't always work out the way I had thought they should. Things will go wrong and get broken and don't always get fixed. Often things can't be put back together as before. I've learned that sometimes things will stay broken and that is OK. I have learned that the best way to get through bad times is thinking about better days or even just moments in the day. I can choose to let go of my limiting stories knowing that I can choose to be loving and loved instead and no longer live out the roles others have tried to place me in.

The fact that you are struggling does not make you a burden. It does not make you unlovable or undesirable or undeserving of love and care. It does not make you too much, too sensitive or too needy. It makes you human. Everyone struggles. Everyone has difficult situations and fall apart at times. However it is not how we fall that's important but how we pick ourselves back up. During these times we weren't always easy to be around one hundred percent of the time. You may sometimes be unpleasant or difficult. You may lash out and say or do things that make the people around you feel sad, helpless and confused, but that is not who you are and don't discount your worth as a human being. The truth is that you can be struggling and still be loved. You can be difficult and still be cared for. You can be less than perfect and still be deserving of compassion and kindness.

Chapter Fourteen
Religion.

Our Religions and Our Beliefs:

In Ireland we have many traditions surrounding death and bereavement. We also have many beliefs and interpretations of a superhuman controlling power. Despite our different religions and a personal God, our collective worship is surprisingly similar. Some people would argue that religious brand names like Catholic or Protestant are no more than different originations all with their own unique promises and selling points.

In recent years we now welcome people with different religious views and some with none into our communities. For the most part people here ascribe to either belong to the Roman Catholic community or the Reformed Protestant Faith, who all share believe in resurrection to eternal life and the committal of the body to the earth from which it came.

In more recent times we have accepted cremation and believe it offers no obstacle to resurrection to eternal life. Some fundamental Christians believe that they will be raptured into heaven leaving behind everyone else who doesn't uphold the truth of the Scriptures.

Humanism:

In recent times more people are living their lives without belief in a God or afterlife. They don't share religious or superstitious beliefs and choose not to participate in religious communities.

Humanists seek to make the best of this one and only life by accepting full responsibility for creating and taking responsibility for their actions. They are happy to share a human morality but without any religious symbols. For humanists death is final and all they would want is their lives to have been a lasting influence on those who remain.

Judaism:

'When Bad Things Happen to Good People' is a book written by Dr Harold Samuel Kushner (1935 - 2023). Dr Kushner was an American Rabbi, author and lecturer. He gained widespread recognition for his ability to simplify complex theological ideas for both Jewish and non-Jewish readers.

'When Bad Things Happen to Good People' became a worldwide best seller and dealt with the death of his son Aaron. The book deals directly with the question of human suffering. Kushner aimed to assist individuals in maintaining their belief in God's benevolence despite experiencing personal tragedies.

He believed that God's love was unconditional, that God may not have the power to prevent suffering but provides solace to those who are affiliated when we bring our pain to God.

How Judaism Approaches Death:

The Jewish faith believes that life is the integration of soul and body into a single entity. Death is the dissolution of body and soul into two separate entities from one. The true self is eternal and unchanging distinct from the physical body. Like Christianity they believe that body will disintegrate but the soul is indestructible.

Also for the body death is not the end and in the resurrection of the dead the soul will be joined to a divinely perfect body. The

Jewish faith has a commandment to bury their dead without delay as a mark of reverence for the dead. Jews are allowed to mourn but not show despair due to the loss of this individual from our lives. Jews believe that death is a temporary and reversible state, a stage of life, not its destination.

Muslim Beliefs:

Muslims believe that life and death are in God's hands and that God appoints a time for each person to pass from this existence into the next. Muslims are reminded regularly that death is inevitable and that the actions of this life determine one's status in the hereafter. When a person dies, his or her relatives are urged to be patient and accepting of God's decree.

It is permissible to cry and express grief at the death of a loved one, though grieving may never fully end, the period of outward mourning typically lasts no more than three days. According to the Qur'an every human is bound to experience death, and we test you (all) through the bad and the good (things of life) by way of trial and on to us you must return.(Qur'an 21/35). For Muslims, burial represents a human being's return to the most elemental state, since we were fashioned from earth by the creator. Thus cremation, preservation of the body, interment in above-ground mausoleums or other methods are not allowed in Islam. Many scholars have indicated that organ donation is permissible in Islam, and is considered a profound charitable act.

Christianity:

The thought of dying and being forgotten or treated like you never existed is a very frightening concept. For those who believe in the Christian religion and have faith will have the promise that we can overcome death, because in death our soul or spirit will continue on. Religion is popular because all religions promise to overcome death in one way or another. Death has no sting for those who believe. Their faith is an absolute truth in a just world and their passing is nothing more than the journey home.

Any suffering is temporary in comparison to what awaits you in the afterlife. It is not surprising that a belief in an afterlife should be an important part of the Christian tradition. If our lives extend beyond the grave the question still remains concerning the nature of what's in store for us on the other side.

There are various Christian views about heaven and hell but they essentially boil down to the following; good people going to heaven as a deserved reward for a virtuous life and bad people will go to hell as a just punishment for an immoral life. In that way the scales of justice are sometimes thought to balance. The views about hell in particular include very different ideas about free will and its role in determining a person's ultimate destiny, with very different views about the nature of moral responsibility and punishment.

Buddhism:

For Buddhists the concern about where you will go when you die is not the important factor, it is important that you are reborn and become someone completely different. The idea of rebirth has been around for a long time even before it was adopted by the Buddhist religion. Buddhists believe that how you behave in this life sets conditions for your later lives.

They see death as just another part of their journey and continuation from life to life. This helps them move away from the fear of death as Christians know it to be and instead see it as just a new chapter. They will make their death as painless as possible for themselves and family as they believe this will have an impact on their next life.

Atheism:

David Cunningham writes as an atheist:

'As an atheist I do not have belief. A belief is by definition not a fact, it is an unproven wish. Living in certain ways because the religious want to gain favour with their God or wants to avoid her/ his displeasure is one of the atheist's arguments. Atheists naturally do not believe in any form of existence after death. Most people would not suggest that their pets continue to have existence after death and we see no evidence that humans are different. When I die it means that I cease to be.'

(David Cunningham-Green is a member of Atheism UK)

That doesn't mean atheists don't think about death. Like most people an atheist will probably not want to die slowly, in agony or causing distress to those around them. Many atheists claim there is a downside to belief in the afterlife, notably the fear of hell in the Christian religion, burning without being consumed and suffering without dying.

Atheists do not accept that there is an afterlife, so obviously do not fear it. An atheist sees death as a full-stop, so it is the process of dying that matters. Atheists can approach death knowing that their actions aren't for anyone other than themselves and the people they love. That's why for many atheists it's important to make sure their death is comfortable and that it doesn't lead to further suffering or difficulties for loved ones.

For atheists there is no God or Satan. God for them is just a symbol for higher consciousness and Satan is a symbol for the ego. They often use their higher consciousness to overcome their lower ego desires. All scientific findings must be open to criticism and challenge.

Life is meaningless thank God!

The countless times I have been told by clients or colleagues that in the time since their loved one has passed that they feel their life is now meaningless. I have learned over many years that our lives are meaningless. It's our greatest gift that we are born with a blank canvas, and we can paint our life story whatever way we wish, that is our birth gift. We are the masters of our destiny. We get to choose how we are going to deal with the effect of tragedy and loss or success in our life. We can't change what happens in life but our inbuilt development and relationship with our individual beliefs carries with it our ability to choose. This gives us the opportunity to learn and find love and in the most tragic of circumstances, the loss of this love.

Religion and Science:

The relationship between religion and science is the subject of continued debate in philosophy and theology. To what extent are religion and science compatible? Are religious beliefs sometimes conducive to science, or do they inevitably pose obstacles to scientific inquiry? The interdisciplinary field of 'science and religion,' also called *'theology and science,'* aims to answer these and other questions. It studies historical and contemporary interactions between these fields and provides philosophical analyses of how they interrelate.

Science aims to define the evolution and the laws of nature. Religion on the other hand provides a moral guidance and psychological understanding. The relationship between science and religion is complex and cannot be explained.

Chapter Fifteen
Living with Loss.

The loss of a friend, relative or partner can be very traumatic. For those left behind there will be emotional upsets as everyone tries to make sense of this new reality. After the burial or cremation society expects a period of mourning. Some will view it that part of them has died, and mixed into the sadness is a feeling of guilt that you didn't do enough, or could or should have done more to prevent the death. You may ask, *'what am I to do with my sadness?'*

You may begin by using traditional formalities of remembrance like looking at the photo album or setting off to pilgrimages to meaningful places to pay homage to this beautiful soul that has left. In time, but not immediately, you will begin to offer blessings for their new journey as the deceased sails away over the horizon to beyond. Grief can be so intense and no words of consolation seem adequate.

The following is quotation from Victor Hugo's *'Toilers of the Sea,'* adapted by Mike George from his book *'You Can Find Inner Peace.'*

'A ship sails and I stand watching until she fades on the horizon and someone at my side says 'she's gone.' Gone where? Gone from my side that is all; she is just as large as when I saw her. The diminished size and total loss of sight, are in me, not in her. And just at the moment when someone at my side says 'she's gone,' there are others who are watching her coming and other voices take up the glad shout 'there she comes!' And that is dying.'

Grief and Survival - The Death Experience:
(Adapted from ' *The Courage to Grieve* 'by Judy Tatelbaum)

The experience of losing a loved one can be painful and will often result in the way we live our lives to change completely. Our outlook and world view will change and our perspective on life will alter beyond all recognition. This time our lives will become very frightening. Our pain will make us search and question for answers. Our relationship with the one who has passed will change also. This experience will force us out from our initial denial and transport us to a new unexamined experience changing our values and our attitudes by setting us on a new course far from the pre-conceived lifestyle we took for granted. The death experience will result in a major turning point in our life and in the lives of those left behind. What we were or thought and how we lived our lives is forced to change and can distort our whole perspective on life, beyond all recognition.

This experience can be very intimidating and force us to search for answers. Once again we will be forced to look at our relationship with the deceased. They will be forever frozen in a photograph, never changing or getting older. This experience will catapult us from a comfortable life and transport us into unimagined new experiences which force us to change our attitudes and setting us on a new course from our pre-conceived idea of where we belong in our world.

To survive we must embrace this new normal. We will need a great deal of assistance and a good network of friendships. If your loss is of a spouse or life partner then self-care is critical and you will need help to endure your pain and assist you in feelings of sadness, anger, loneliness, despair and neediness. We will need help in expressing our emotions. We must find ways to let go of the pain if only for a short time. Even before we begin to make sense of our emotions we will most likely go through a wide range

139

of experiences. The first stage is disbelief and hope for reunion. This can last for days or weeks and is eventually given up slowly. *'I just can't believe it,'* is often the first reaction. You will feel everything is unreal and a sense of hopeless. You can find yourself in a state of unreality and be only just aware of what is going on around you. These responses are both natural and nature's way of protecting you from the full impact and the shock all at once. It also protects you from blind panic and will ease you unknowingly into a position of reality over your loss.

The next experience can be uncontrolled anger, sometimes it's irrational responses and refusal to accept the circumstances and events of the passing. When we slowly begin to emerge from this trance, the enormity and finality of the loss becomes real. If you are fortunate you may begin to share tears and ruminate over the details along with memories from the past and unfulfilled ambitions and dreams.

We will feel unprepared to cope with our emotions and unable to deal with the tasks at hand. During this time we may be unable to relate to family and friends causing us to withdraw from society. We can suffer complete loss in our confidence and experience extreme fatigue. The type of tiredness we encounter is not the type that sleep can sooth or replenish our minds or bodies.

All of the above symptoms are only temporary. The essential thing to remember is that you have never experienced this before and our brains are unable to assimilate or make sense of all that has happened. Every morning you will awake and for a few moments be unaware that you must face the day knowing that your heartbreak is real and nothing is going to change. During this phase when life has no real meaning you can hold thoughts of suicide when you feel your life has nothing to offer either to yourself or anyone. These intrusive thoughts will disappear in time and we will discuss suicide and suicidal thoughts in a later chapter.

Panic Attacks as a result of Bereavement:

For no apparent reason you may feel that you are having a nervous breakdown. These unexamined and unexplainable feelings can arrive unannounced like an unwelcome, uninvited visitor who arrives at your door during times of major stress. To complicate this further they can arrive during times of relative calm too, like eating with friends or just watching TV.

The panic can be a product of direct involvement in a bereavement or any number of other stressful situations dating back for decades, even early childhood experiences that you couldn't understand at the time can bubble to the surface. The symptoms differ and no two people will experience the exact same sensations. The symptoms will often include feelings of your heart racing or having palpitations making you think you are having a heart attack, dizzy feelings and blurred vision, light-headedness, sweating with a fever, and a need to sit or lay down to avoid fainting. They can also cause anxious and irrational thinking or a strong feeling of dread, danger or foreboding. You can feel unable to join in a conversation and feel fear over making a fool of yourself running the risk of looking stupid and drawing unwanted attention to yourself.

These are all very common symptoms and while potentially paralysing at the time are nothing to worry about as with treatment they can be eradicated. Sometimes just thinking about an event is enough to trigger a panic attack or just when you are dropping off to sleep you are also very susceptible. Having severe panic attacks can lead to irrational fears and untreated can eventually lead on to phobias. If you are nursing someone very close to you whose death is expected, their absence in your life can be an unbearable prospect, or the death resulted from a major incident causing numerous deaths which can be too much for you to comprehend. These are all triggering events which the human brain has difficulties processing. At first, panic attacks can be mild and only display modest changes like a tingling sensation. You may experience a sudden change in body temperature or shortness of breath. This may be only a once off experience or the beginning of a more vicious cycle. Sometimes trying to avoid these attacks can create more panic, thus creating a negative feedback loop.

Your efforts to avoid these panic events begin to impact on your day to day life experience. Doctors and therapists will sometimes recommend anti-anxiety medication. Research has shown that knowledge is power and as human beings we have evolved to cope with any and all adversities in life. For example, suppose we eat something that is off, our bodies will induce us to vomit it out of our system or our bowels will excrete by causing us to have a bout of diarrhoea.

While these symptoms can be extremely unpleasant they are our body's natural way of keeping us safe, much in the same way our bodies make us faint slowly to avoid a straight fall to the ground. If your doctor prescribes medication it may be for the short term to help you cope. Our fight or flight responses from our hunter/ gatherer days are still only just under the surface of our natural responses. At the onset of a panic attack your body has the same reaction as if you were falling off a building or being chased by an angry Rottweiler, our bodies will automatically go into survival mode. Adrenalin is pumped at speed around our bodies and our mouths can go dry causing us to feel nauseated and dizzy. We can feel ill and shake while some can be highly aroused due to an unimaginable level of danger.

This is the body's natural reaction to fear whether real or imagined. We can be left bewildered and struggle to make the connection that this is your body doing what is natural to protect itself. The good news is these symptoms can be treated. Begin by saying to yourself, '*do these symptoms serve me any longer?*' Your *'panic'* is usually about an event that has happened to you in the past

142

which obviously you survived, so these thoughts, despite their appearance and severity, are only the echo of the real event that you have already lived through and survived. There is an old saying, *'fear knocked the door and faith answered it, but no one was there.'* If you find yourself troubled by panic attacks remember that its cause is in the past and no matter how real it may seem it is just an illusion. Say to yourself this is just a panic attack which is triggered by an event I have already survived. It can't harm me any more than it already has!

Gradually these attacks will lose their grip on your life. It's important to always ask yourself, *'is what I am thinking really true?'* and sit quietly and wait for a feeling rather than an answer. If your panic attacks are regular and serious then medical intervention may be necessary but often self-examination can be sufficient. You can begin with using a journal and writing in detail the date and nature of the panic feelings. Ask yourself what was happening when the panic attack struck. What was happing in your day up to and until the panic arrived. When you see patterns and/or triggers in your behaviour it makes it much easier to change or avoid these triggers moving forward.

Fearing Changes:

We may not want to think about loss but during our lifetime it's going to become part of our experience of life.

We fear change and the way we do things. What seemed like science fiction yesterday wouldn't raise an eyebrow today. We are all experiencing major changes and challenges. Our high value skills are becoming displaced by automation. Our relying on experts is giving way to Artificial Intelligence. Most of our lives we look to others for advice and reassurance. During the COVID pandemic we witnessed our world leaders and politicians fumble, and found them to be totally out of control. Our news media that we pay a license fee which is supposed to be impartial is now reduced to following ratings and trading impartiality for popularity and pressure from politicians. What has happened to us is like when we were at school and the teacher leaves the room. In a very short space of time the class descends into total chaos. When the teacher doesn't return we are faced with loss as we know no-one is coming to restore order in our lives and the person we looked to for their solid reassurance is gone. We are frightened beyond words and others are now turning to us for support and reassurance. Now we must rise to the challenges of life and make difficult decisions to navigate our way through the labyrinth of hard choices and invent a new normal.

You don't need to have all the answers. Take your time and take time for yourself. Try to begin with creating realistic goals for what to do next. Don't be afraid to look for help and support from friends. Focus only on the day and where possible do not spend time looking back into the past or projecting into the future. Take time to assess the situation and grieve and allow yourself to feel angry at the changes that are thrust upon you that you never contemplated. Try to build a small network of allies who can offer you some inspiration and practical guidance and provide you with some resources when required. This is not a time to doubt yourself, no matter how difficult things appear. Believe in your innate ability to rise out of the ashes of destruction.

Covid:

The first human outbreak of Covid 19 occurred in Wuhan, People's Republic of China on the 17th November 2019. The World Health Organisation declared the outbreak on the 30th January 2020 and it was classed as a pandemic on the 11th March 2020. The number of deaths recorded are estimated to be in excess of three million people worldwide. When the numbers are finally all accounted for it is believed it could be in excess of 15 million, according to a BBC news report in May 2022. For us as individuals living in the United Kingdom and Ireland we found ourselves totally unprepared for the scale of the pandemic. Our government and those we depended on to protect us seemed to be equally as unprepared and unable to deal with the scale of the events when we were looking to them the most for reassurance.

Some politicians even took advantage of the situation for personal gain. Our health care system was poorly prepared to weather the storm with too few staff, too few beds and hospitals that were ineffective for infection control. This along with staffing shortages led to a breakdown in dealing with the infection.

Lockdowns were announced from the 23th March and people could only leave their homes for essential reasons like buying food and exercise.

Covid totally changed family life, including employment and financial security, family wellbeing and education. As usual those at the bottom of the economic scale suffered much more stress than those belonging to middle or upper class families. Social distancing was introduced as a means to slow down the rate of infection.

Locally our hospitals and nursing homes maintained a compassionate approach and tried to find a balance to allow the dying person to spend precious time with their loved ones but many were denied access because of the rules and risk of infection. Spiritual and emotional support could not always be provided and healthcare guidance had to be adhered to. Internet and virtual communication were of little comfort to those who just wanted to be face to face with their loved ones at the end of life. These precious moments were stolen from us denying many the chance to say goodbye.

The pandemic changed death rituals and left grieving families without a sense of closure. It took away any comfort to grieving family and friends. The added trauma of not having the opportunity to be with our loved ones when they were dying during Covid will have a lasting impact on those left behind. The feeling of isolation and not being allowed to grieve with family and friends is traumatic beyond words.

Wakes and funeral service attendance numbers were dictated by government regulations depending on what stage of lockdown we were at. Some families had to endure their loved ones being removed by the undertaker and buried alone with no one present at the funeral. Others had to restrict numbers, sometimes to single digits. It is a heartbreaking task to decide which 15 people can attend your partner's funeral. I witnessed this first hand with a close friend who told me of how difficult this task was as well as the priest providing the Last Rites from outside their bedroom window.

Because these events were so commonplace during this time it is hard for people to own up to it as being traumatic, they feel selfish because why should they complain when so many went through the same or worse. However we have to remember that grief affects us all differently and we should not be ashamed to seek help or speak to someone about these feelings.

If you were bereaved during Covid and the lockdown you may not have had any real opportunity to share your grief due to the restrictions. The chance to avail of the support from family, friends and the community was taken from you. This can lead to longer pain and suffering. The feeling that you were unable to protect your loved one, especially if they died alone in hospital or a care home, and you being prevented from sharing their final moments. Your grief has most likely been unrecognised by society.

Having a minimal funeral service and no real opportunity to say goodbye or draw a loving relationship to a final close will make your job of rebuilding even more challenging. The Canadian poet and writer Ann Michaels wrote:

"Grief, loss and regret are not the end of the story. They are the middle of the story. There is a huge amount to see, to hear, to understand, and to do in order for us to reach the end of the story and find meaning in it."

Death by Suicide:

The worst goodbyes are the ones where you didn't get a chance to say goodbye. You will never forget the last time you saw them and their memory will haunt you for a long time. People don't commit suicide, they die by suicide. The human mind is like a Rubik's cube. If the colours come together in the right combination then we can be at risk and end our lives without any lengthy preparation. On the other hand it can be meticulously planned to the last detail. Either way the person who decides to end their existence sees this as an exit strategy out of unbearable pain and confusion. Their last day now becomes your worst day and if you can't imagine the pain and desolation then consider yourself extremely fortunate.

This type of passing is both heartbreaking and traumatic. You may have often been afraid that this was a possibility and now your worst fear has happened. On the other hand they may as well have been brutally murdered, and in some respect they were. If you can imagine that they had a heart attack in their brain and just like a heart attack in our chest we have little or no control of how or when we have to experience this unwelcome tragic event. People never really choose to leave. I know it's hard to explain but sometimes the voices inside our heads are guilty of murder.

Sometimes no matter how much we fight the only way out is taking the ultimate irreversible decision, so great is the pain and utter desolation. In your pain please remember, their death will leave heartache that no one, or no length of time can heal. But in the fullness of time love will leave memories that no one can steal.

This type of passing will have a major impact, not just on the nearest and dearest of the deceased but also on friends, colleagues and the local community. I will try to list the common community response and feel free to add some of your own as well.

1. After the initial shock you may feel anger with the person because you know that love, and love alone, should have been enough to save them. This acute stage will stay and for a time can increase. We can struggle in trying to find a sense of meaning in our grief. We feel we are in danger in losing our place in the world.

2. We can feel a very heavy sense of rejection and a sense of finality which can never be undone or changed.

3. We can experience feelings that are totally outside our control. Nothing in our lives can ever prepare us for this situation.

4. You may wonder how much pain and suffering they had to endure alone and felt they could not share with you. What were their last thoughts and did they think of you? Why was the unconditional love you shared not enough for them to stay?

5. You may feel some relief now that the worst has happened that they are no longer in pain and your worry about if and when it might happen has disappeared.

6. Along with your anger, a sense of shame may invade your grief depending on your faith. Was this a sinful act? A sense

of embarrassment or stigma can also arise due to the fact that society allows and puts on you and your family their religious or cultural views on suicide.

7. You may have the added burden of dealing with suspicion and blame. If the death has occurred in the home then it's now treated as a crime scene, and you are questioned and treated like a suspect until eliminated from any inquiry. You are expected to understand the need for a post-mortem and an inquest with no heed for the intrusion into your private life. This is such a different starting place for our grief.

You will wonder why this has happened and how you or anyone else was unable to prevent it happening. You think you should have seen changes leading up to the event. Once a person has made up their mind to end their life they can feel a secret sense of relief. If they have a date or exit plan in place then often they are more relaxed and display a more settled persona. When the event does happen it's often more unbelievable given their settled demeanour.

Different family members will grieve differently. Some will refuse to mention the deceased and refuse to take part in any public type of mourning, refusing all offers of support. You can feel such a sense of loss when you have to let go of the physical body knowing they will never return. At times you will feel struck in your grief and for the most part feel that life for you now is no longer worth living.

You will wrestle with your loss and for the most part continue to carry on with the necessities of life thinking that you will never be able to work on your grief. You might try going back to work if only on a phased return. There will be days when you will struggle, and friends who found you fine yesterday will wonder what they said or did to upset you. A careless remark or snide comment can feel like a dagger to the heart and send you back to square one when all they did was ask thoughtless questions thinking that such a tragedy could never happen in their world.

Statistically one person in four will be affected by this type of experience and more often than not it is a question of when rather than if. In time the thick fog of grief will begin to clear and the painful journey will give way to small parts of your days when you can experience a sense of normality. You will learn again that the sun did shine even on your worst day, it was just that you were too busy trying to cope to even notice. Please resist from telling survivors what they should have done and don't tell survivors what you would've done. When the funeral is over and everyone's gone home where do you go? Everyone came to pay their respects but you are the one left with your life in a mess with countless unanswered questions and no answers. This is the time you must give yourself compassion, the type of compassion you would give anyone in a similar situation. Remember the guilt feelings you are suffering at the moment are not a life sentence.

Try to see this event as totally out of your control. Think of all the things you could have or should have done and write them down no matter how difficult this is. Write a journal and only put down how you feel at this date and time. If you don't they will form a loop in your head and deny you any peace. Consider writing a letter or several letters to the deceased about anything and everything you need to say. You can keep these in a memory box, have a ritual by reading them aloud or bury/burn them as you see fit. Dispose of them in whatever way eases the pain of the guilt that has invaded your personal space. Then decide to have at least a few guilt free moments.

If you keep your guilt free moments until last thing before you sleep at night it greatly increases the chance of your new day opening a small window allowing a chink of light into your very dark place. In your small window of light ask yourself is the life sentence I have imposed on myself really a fair judgement. Ask yourself, where do my barriers of non-forgiveness to myself come from? Are they the product of my childhood upbringing or my religious/cultural background and why am I choosing to hold on to my guilt? Are these beliefs serving or hindering me in my grief? In order to heal am I able to let some very deep ingrained beliefs go in order to allow my life to move forward?

You are not God and you can't love someone enough to force them to survive. We don't have the power to change these events and will continue to suffer if we don't realise we couldn't have done anything to stop this even if we knew. Allow yourself permission to have the pain come through you, but in the understanding that what you knew at the time was all you had and no one has the gift of hindsight. Don't ever feel bad about making a decision about your own life that may upset others. You are not responsible for their happiness. You are responsible for your own happiness. Anyone who expects you to continue to live a life of misery for their happiness is using your grief for their benefit. Give serious consideration for allowing such people to continue to be in your life.

Chapter Sixteen
Faith.

What Should you Believe:

As we discussed earlier, everyone's experience of bereavement is unique. Prior to this experience you may have had no difficulties with the concept of having a religious faith. You may now be furious with God that he allowed something like this to happen and your faith may be totally shattered. Or perhaps your faith stood you in good stead and has sustained you in your darkest hour. Some people have found that their experience has broken the unwritten contract with God, for as long as they believe and keep the rules of their Church then this tragic event should not have happened. They will feel that God has let them down. Their belief in a just world has been shattered while for others however, it was this experience of unimaginable loss and utter desolation that turned them on to a higher power and found belief in God the like of which they would never have had without the loss experience.

'When we are faced with disaster we have a choice. We can see the disaster as it is or we can create a fantasy about it that aims to protect us from the full horror of what has happened. When the disaster we face is the death of someone we love, the circumstances of that person's death might allow us to create the fantasy that the person has not died. We might tell ourselves that the person who has given us the news has been given the wrong name, or our loved one had failed to catch the plane that has crashed. Bereavement counsellors know this to be the first stage of bereavement and call it denial, giving us time to gather strength and courage.'
(Dorothy Rowe – ' *What Should I Believe?*')

'After the funeral and everyone's gone home. Where do you go?
It was like a big reception and everybody came,
But I was left with the mess. I was left with me.'

(Benjamin Allen)

'Don't die with your dead.'

(Anonymous)

'Did you know that when you cry for your dead,
You cry for you and not them?
You cry because you lost them,
because you don't have them by your side.
You think it all ends in death.
And you're also thinking they don't exist anymore.
So if your dead are gone, where are they?
Yes they have left, or they are not in another place.
Is that place better that this?
Yes definitely that place is better than this.
So why do we suffer for their departure?

(Anonymous)

'When you have finished accepting that they are no longer here,
but that they are in another place. A place where they are no longer
sick or suffering. Then you will stop mourning them and you'll get
back the good memories so they keep accompanying you with the
joy of that you've lived.

If you truly loved them, love again and this time with greater
strength, with greater purity.
I respect your pain, and the way you express it.
I know you cry without comfort.
But today I say to you.
Don't die with your dead.

153

Remember we only see one side of the coin.
We are not looking the other way,
We are not seeing the wonderful place of light where they stand.
What if we start seeing death as a second birth?
A second birth we all go through.

Don't die with your dead. Honour them by living your life as they would have wanted you to. Let them transcend, and you keep living.'

(Rev. Sydney Callaghan – 'Good Grief' Adapted)

'Jesus Wept:'

The shortest verse in the Bible encapsulates the human response of a man of strength brought to a situation of distress. In our Western cultures displays of feelings by men are still generally considered a taboo or out of place. For a woman to cry is permissible, but not for a man. It conflicts with the macho image expected of the male of the species. But why should this be?

There is therapy in tears. A doctor writing of this drew attention to the statistical fact of female longevity over men, he speculated on the possibility of women living longer being due to their greater willingness to cry than men. In shedding of tears there's not only a release of tension but also of a toxic component. Instead of shoving the grief poison down into the system, it is being released. Men, he says, with their reluctantly to shed tears can cause serious damage to their health.

The Irish Wake:

It is still a common custom to have a wake in Ireland. A wake involves family and friends keeping watch over the body of the deceased, usually in the home of the person but more recently sometimes a funeral home is used with allotted times set aside to view the remains and comfort the bereaved. It is a way for family and friends to share their feelings and memories of the deceased. The name wake is thought to have originated in the 1900s because of unknown diseases causing someone to appear dead. As the family began to mourn the perceived passed would awaken. For this reason the body was kept in the deceased home for at least one night. Traditionally windows of a wake house are left open to allow the soul of the person to leave, mirrors are covered and clocks are stopped as a mark of respect. In the Roman Catholic tradition candles are burned for the duration of the wake to symbolically guide the deceased soul on its forward journey.

Prayers are often recited and memorable times are recounted. The wake can be cathartic and provide a wonderful opportunity to allow neighbours and friends to show sympathy and support. It also allows the family to repeat the story of how the deceased passed, continuously helping them to somehow make sense of their loss.

It is important to reflect on the good memories with the deceased by viewing the corpse and allowing physical handshakes and hugs to support the bereaved family. For some people they feel unable to partake in these rituals and don't want their homes to be a place for the public to arrive uninvited. Sometimes we don't want others to witness our vulnerability and sensitivity. In our experience of loss we can both feel deeply hurt and greatly healed. At our worst we can hate the term loss as if we have misplaced someone in an act of gross carelessness. On the other side of this we can experience small gestures of recognition and thoughtfulness that can mean so much in our distress. Expressions of kindness are not measured by their deeds but in terms of thoughtfulness. So much can be accomplished by that thoughtful note or visit. Often just your presence in sharing your time can mean so much when we are lost in our grief.

One of the best gifts to the bereaved is your willingness to let them talk about their loss. People mistakenly say you will only upset yourself by continually talking about it but more accurately it means you will upset me if you do! To top it off you can find yourself submerged in trivial conversation from anything like weather and holidays. You may, out of politeness, have to endure pointless conversations when inside your heart is screaming with heartache and a sense of sadness tears cannot soothe. When at the same time your insides are screaming, do you not see my pain and why should you expect me to smile through this triviality and patronising tones of pity when my world is ending? In addition to these feelings expect the view that I shouldn't laugh when I am bereaved, it isn't respectful. Laughter can be very therapeutic. It can help release tension and is often the very part of our learning to cope.

Sometimes it is good to laugh in the face of tragedy and life's absurdities especially if the person who has died had liked to laugh and enjoyed your sense of humour. Beginning to try to enjoy life, especially events and familiar experiences you would have shared, can be a very bittersweet experience, both comforting and distressing at the same time. The longing to share it with the person who has died underlines the pain of their absence. But your courage to try to enjoy in the pain of their absence is an affirmation and celebration of the real meaning of life and your willingness to risk this heartache both for your memory and healing. This anonymous verse comes to mind.

'Though I am dead, laugh and be glad for all that life is giving, And I, though dead, will share your joy in living.'

Sometimes when we lose someone close we can begin to appreciate a new zest for life as your experience creates a new awareness of your own mortality. The fact that life can and will end so suddenly makes you more inclined to live in present moments.

156

Chapter Seventeen
Sorting out Stuff:
Don't Make Grief your Lifetimes Work.

In the absence of our loved one we are sooner or later going to have to decide how we move on. We will have to decide what to dispose of and what we will hold on to. There is no right or wrong way or right or wrong time to do this, just whenever you feel ready. It is often the simplest reminders that are the most difficult to move on from. Sometimes decisions are out of your control by having to move house or return home may force you into making decisions about the personal items that were part and parcel of your loved ones life. Some people believe that by holding on to items of a personal nature that you haven't or are unable to move on.

A very dear friend who lost his wife after a long illness would place her night dress sprayed with her favourite perfume on the bed to imagine she was still with him when he slept. He would have been embarrassed to tell his family but I assured him it was just a way to help soothe him and was a lovely idea. Only you can judge when the right time is to tackle practical matters. Please do not bow to pressure and never allow anyone to make these decisions for you. Find a relative or friend who knows how difficult it is letting go and dismantling the life you loved so much to help you.
I've often said to clients that your loved one was so much more than possessions. I know that by looking at a pair of old shoes or a coat hanging in the wardrobe is of no use to anyone but you somehow can feel their presence. Sometimes passing more usable items on to people who knew the deceased and would treasure

157

them would help or perhaps think about donating to a local charity shop. Better to choose a shop not in your own locality to avoid a painful memory coming to life when you could see someone else wearing a favourite item of clothing.

Only you can make these very difficult decisions and you also have to consider other members of your family. In the beginning we can fool ourselves that our loved one is coming back but the reality is they are never coming back and the comfort of having constant reminders can easily be overcome by feelings of loss. Some people, in an effort to avoid the reality, will make very significant changes very early into the grief journey and often have serious regrets later on. We can do this to avoid the pain of the loss but we have to grieve now or later, we cannot ignore it forever, but it's a journey we must make in order to come to terms with our loss. I have known people to have some favourite items recycled into cushions or stuffed toys and given to family and close friends. Not knowing what to do would indicate to me that you should not do anything yet because when you do know you will be able to carry out these decisions as and when is right for you. Always be kind and never judge yourself harshly and try not to bottle up your emotions.

Learning to Move On:

This could now be the time to learn to put yourself first. You might say, *'I can't put myself first, all my life I was always at the service of others. I am used to putting others first. I have been used to going without for too long. I spent my life going along to get along.'*

Life will not define you by what you have done but what you have become. Courage does not always roar. It can be a quiet voice at the end of the day, *'try again.'*

Can you find Love Again after being Widowed?
'Time is limited so don't waste it on others opinions.'

(Steve Jobs)

Stop looking for someone to complete you, stop expecting that someone will come into your life making everything all right. No one can bring you anything that you do not already possess, by that I mean our idea of happiness and sense of belonging. I would encourage you to never look back at your life with regret or anger, what's done is done. Instead look forward with hope and expectation because every new day is an opportunity to start again. You may have never thought about it but your greatest teacher can be your greatest loss.

Great learning can come from your experience, you got through your darkest moments even when you thought you would never see past the sorrow, take strength from that. If everything we did in life was easy and everything worked out as planned, then we would never learn anything. It is in our moments of absolute and utter despair that we can really learn something profound about ourselves. These experiences, although extremely painful, are the contrast of life and if we are open to learn and make new memories then anything is possible and it is possible to find love again.

Grief takes time to heal, but the length of time you take is absolutely at your discretion. Finding a new partner can be a wonderful experience and while it does not and will not ever replace the love you had for your previous partner, I would always say that if you find true love once in your life, then you can find it again. These are very personal and emotional decisions. Some may never marry again but might be open to the possibility of a new relationship. There will always be guilt issues to deal with at the outset of a new relationship. New relationships can be complicated. Often you can feel like you're trying to live up to the standards set by your former spouse or your new partner can feel they are living in their shadow. It reminds me of the joke of when a man was walking his dog along the graveyard, and he could hear the cries of a man kneeling at a grave sobbing uncontrollably saying, *'Oh why did you have to die, why did you have to die?'* As the tears were running down his face the man gently asked was that your wife that died? The reply was, *'no it was my partner's first husband.'*

Try to ensure that your new partner will be able to handle the fact that you or both of you have been married before and will continue to allow yourselves to discuss their previous spouse and lifestyles without feeling a sense of threat. You need to set boundaries at the outset giving each other enough space to allow your new relationship to grow. If you had to nurse your partner for a considerable amount of time, then maybe your relationship would have changed and your role in the relationship became one of a care giver near the end. After your bereavement you can easily find yourself looking for someone else to care for and this can easily lead to a co-dependency relationship. You both may have children to consider, and their approval or disapproval may factor in the relationship.

The most important part is getting to know each other first, and if you decide you want to make more permanent arrangements then you can proceed slowly. Your new partner should never be your therapist and your grief should only be discussed in detail with your counsellor, therapist or close trusted circles of friends. Your relationship will come under undue stress if you both continue to talk nonstop about your past partners. Always be open and honest in your discussion but don't overshare as this can be interpreted by the new partnership as being compared to or overshadowed by the previous relationship. When a marriage ends in a bereavement, quite often your circle of friends changes also. This is not often deliberate but it's never going to be the same again and we can feel that we no longer fit in the same way we would have done with the same friends group as in the past.

Before getting serious about your new partner decide what you would like from your new relationship. You may be looking for a different type of person or relationship, or perhaps a similar personality to the one that you lost. Letting go of guilt is difficult, and remember it is possible to love more than one person in your life and you can if you desire to have a successful relationship after losing your partner. Don't be afraid of self-reflection. Take time to consider how your life may have changed since the loss of your partner. You may have thought that you could never find a meaningful relationship again. You may have made a promise never to allow yourself to be open to the possibility of meeting a new partner out of a sense of respect.

In my personal journey I was fortunate that my partner gave me her blessing to meet someone and rebuild my life again. I have known many others whose partners weren't as accommodating and forbid them to ever seek a new life again. I would suggest that often people who are facing an end of life prognosis can be so afraid that they want to hold on to the life as they know it. It is more about fear than any rule or instruction that can never be changed or amended. Your siblings, children and sometimes even parents can have strong opinions about your new relationship.

While some might be very supportive, not everyone will approve. This may be due to a sense of fear of losing their connection to you or missing out on a possible future inheritance. They may also feel that you are vulnerable and run the risk of being taken advantage of. You have a duty not to let your new relationship cloud your judgement. Just proceed with caution. If your nearest and dearest are all saying the same thing however then you should definitely listen to them and at least reevaluate the relationship before making any major decisions.

Eventually you may consider allowing your new partner into your home or leaving your home to go and live with your new partner.

For some this would not be an issue but for others it could be a deal breaker in so far as they couldn't share the same home that they had previously shared with their former partner. These decisions should be taken slowly, and with great sensitivity. Some may insist in a complete new and fresh start with none of the trappings of the previous relationship. If both parties agree then there is no issue, but one may be unable to give up the family home because of any number of reasons including financial or sentimental ties. I would always encourage my clients to perhaps wait at least a year before making any serious lifestyle decisions. The old saying, 'decide in haste and repent at leisure,' comes to mind. If you both have children, they must be considered and included in any formal decisions.

Both partners are going to struggle in learning to love again. You may encounter push back from your children or your partner's, and potential new friends may not welcome you as you wished. Remember it's not about what others are going to think, it's about what you and your partner want from life and if you can bring each other happiness in a new relationship. The greatest gift we can give our children is our experience of happiness. Some day your children are going to figure you out. I promise you they will. The type of parent you are. The type of spouse you are. How you treat other people. How much effort you put into them.

'The right partner will not complete you. You are already whole. The right partner will expand you. They will catalyse your growth and elevate your consciousness'

(Anonymous)

'Happiness isn't a destination you arrive at some day. It's a destination you make every day. It's choosing to see the beauty in the world, the love in your heart and the potential in each moment.'

(Unknown)

Breaking Through Limitations:

One of our greatest fears is our beginning to break through our grief. We fear that our actions will hurt or betray our loved ones. Sometimes these thoughts and feelings are unfounded. We can often imagine that our new decisions are not going to meet with the approval of other significant people in our lives and we fear their disapproval. These negative thoughts have the potential to hold us in a very dark place. We can fear losing the good opinions of others so much that we prevent ourselves from rebuilding our lives in meaningful ways. We can torture ourselves with thoughts that our new beginning will hurt others to the extent that we can just shut down for fear of upsetting others.

We must make decisions about making new connections and decide if our changing will meet with approval of family and friends. You may have to decide if your changing is upsetting to others because it impacts on them and their relationship with you. This is because they don't want you to change the boundaries of your relationship with them. Sometimes our family and friends will have your best intentions for you and sometimes it's for their benefit. Never be afraid to question others knowing what is best for you. These are your choices and we must learn to own our decisions. Taking ownership of this is both freeing and scary.

Letters from an Empath: Learning Through Grief:

(Unknown)

I have learned through my grief that I am not responsible for managing your emotions. I am finished walking on eggshells or telling you what you want to hear in order to keep the peace. I am no longer an emotional sponge. From now on my responsibility is to myself to learn to heal my own wounds and practice self-care. My plan is in maintaining healthy boundaries especially with those who are unhealthy.

163

I have learned that I cannot change people no matter how much I think they need to change. My spiritual awaking is not about owning crystals, doing yoga, or chanting mantras. I have let my higher power connect with my grief to expand my consciousness so I can experience my highest potential and feel the joy in becoming fully human and fully alive. Before Nelson Mandela left his prison he recited these words.

'As I stand before this door to my freedom, I realise that if I do not leave my pain, anger and bitterness behind me, I will still be in prison. How many of us have imprisoned ourselves inside the walls of anger and bitterness. Holding grudges does not make you strong. It makes you bitter. Forgiveness does not make you weak, it sets you free. Don't imprison yourself forever.'

Nelson Mandela

Organ Donation:

Although the law around organ donation has changed to an opt-out system in many parts of the UK, your family will still be consulted if organ donation is a possibility. Your family will be informed and reassured that their loved one is being kept alive by artificial means. All tests are showing brain death has occurred and they are asked to allow their loved ones organs to be donated to help save the life of others.

No one can imagine the pain, anguish, distress and emotionally challenging decision placed on the next of kin and whole family. Even though the wishes of the donor can be very clear, and it's obvious the donor is being kept alive by the use of ventilator and artificial means, they are still alive and the family's hopes for a miracle are now dashed. We cling to the hope that where there is breath there is life. For these families the grieving process begins when the donor is still technically alive. For organ donation to be successful, it may be necessary to keep a loved on a life support

164

for an extended period and can cause added suffering. I have met families who have made this decision and have friends who are alive and well today because of the generosity of donors and their families. Knowing the heart of a son, daughter, father or mother, continues to beat on in the chest of someone else can be a comforting experience but won't eliminate the grief that comes from losing someone so tragically.

This chapter only refers to organ donation in relation to authorisation by the donor prior to death or in agreement with the next of kin. There are two types of consent – explicit or presumed consent. As medical science advances the number of people helped by organ donation increases continuously. The demand for organ donation is rising faster than the actual number of donors. Organ donation varies in different countries. The opt-out system applies in Northern Ireland and it basically means that if you haven't registered an objection to organ donation then you will be considered to have no objection to becoming a donor when you die.

If you want to be considered for organ donation in the event of your death it's really important that you talk to your loved ones and make them aware of your decision. It's been my experience that families recover from their grief better when the deceased donor organs are made available for transplant. Family members of brain dead patients experience a unique situation in which they are told that their loved one is dead but are also asked to consider organ donation. This decision is both very complex and stressful for the family of the potential donor as they are facing an unexpected death in an unfamiliar environment, most likely an ICU ward in a hospital. Before considering organ donation the family must accept that the patient is brain dead and further medical treatment would be futile. Organ donation can be a comfort to family members when they are convinced that their decision was correct to authorise the organ donation.

If Not For You:

The following was written by a donor recipient, reprinted with permission and read aloud at a thanksgiving service at the Renal Unit at Omagh Hospital. The author remains anonymous.

'If not for you, there would not be me,
that gift of life you gave me.
There were tears of joy, there were tears of sorrow,
You gave hope for a brighter tomorrow.

I wiped away the tears, tried to cry
I knew someone would live and others die.
The only way I could understand
was to realise it was God's plan.

If not for you what would I do?
God choose someone, he sent you.
Now part of me has thrived, t
hanks to you donor I have survived.

And with each new day, the thought comes through
I would not be alive if not for you.'

(Anonymous)

Chapter Eighteen
Public/Communal Grief.

Public grief will be experienced by many when devastating news of tragedy is announced. Feelings of disbelieve, unfairness, shock, and numbness are but a few of the reactions. Even if we didn't personally know the individuals involved, it does not diminish their importance in our lives. We now live in a social media world with direct access giving the impression that we have a unique relationship with celebrity. This allows us to feel they have a special place in our lives resulting in us experiencing very real emotions of grief. We may think our world will never be the same again. These losses can be a painful reminder of our own past bereavement experiences. Our personal grief can be compounded by knowing that countless others are going through a similar experience.

These events can cause us to experience a reality check in that if it happened to them then it can happen to me too. Saying to someone you didn't even know them and ridiculing them about how they are feeling is not helpful in any way. This type of grief can often be referred to as mourning sickness, described as an emotional and recreational grieving especially when we only knew them for their fame, wealth and beauty. For younger people the loss of a celebrity can challenge their view of the world and a belief that they thought would never change. Often they feel connected to this famous person and the loss can sometimes send a deep sense of loneliness and abandonment. If these symptoms continue for longer than three months and include an out of normal routine and a sense of apathy you should consider seeking some professional help.

Collective Grief and Community Trauma (the Troubles):

For such a small Island we have had a long, difficult and complicated relationship with culture and religion in what we colloquially call the Troubles. These events have cost an untold number of lives, destroying communities and causing division among families, friends and neighbours.

The number of people killed directly is in excess of three and a half thousand but the real number is much greater. Many people have had their lives torn apart by these deaths, dying from broken hearts or never being the same person they were before. Some have ended their lives because they couldn't deal with the loss of their loved ones, for them the pain of their grief was too much to endure. Being from Omagh, I am often reminded of the events of the 15/08/1998.

Unfortunately every town, village, and community has had to deal with loss as a result of the Troubles. This was a period of conflict involving republican and loyalist paramilitaries, the British security forces and civilians. It's not the remit of this book to delve into individual tragic events or why the Troubles started in this part of Ireland other than to reaffirm that no one has the monopoly on pain and loss. All of these losses include disbelief, feeling numb, haunting images or flashbacks, anger, guilt, fear and indescribable pain of loss.

The Good Friday or Belfast Agreement signed on the 10th April 1998 brought us to a place where we could agree to differ on our ideas of sovereignty, restoring self-governance on the basis of power-sharing. We have had countless setbacks but no one would ever want those dark days to return. I am convinced that the years of death and destruction have caused everyone in this place a level of trauma often unrecognisable in ourselves.

The Omagh Bomb (15-08-1998):

Everyone has their own story about this event, and this portion of my book only refers to how a whole community can sometimes be the part of the bereavement process while not directly affected or involved in the situation.

This event is undoubtedly the worst single act of terrorism in the long and bloody history of what we have known as the Troubles; as if somehow we can have a scale of how much people suffer. I am very aware that I am writing this portion of the book almost three decades on from this human massacre. This event happened just when we were beginning to settle into the possibility that we could enjoy some sense of peace and normality with the ink not quite dry yet on the Good Friday/Belfast Agreement. It was only signed and ratified a few months earlier on the 10/04/1998, offering us a new beginning. Omagh suddenly became a home for the world's media who descended on the town as the atrocity became world news.

The scale of this tragedy and its aftermath fall well outside the brief of this book, so I will only touch upon the events briefly. As a town and community we have suffered along with the affected families, not only in their grief but their quest for truth and justice. Omagh, for those who don't know, is a small market town situated about seventy miles west from Belfast at the foot of the Sperrin Mountains with a population of approximately twenty-five thousand people. Omagh was a garrison town and the St Lucia Barracks is now a shared education campus. Omagh is the county town of Tyrone and is a commercial centre for the county. The town is situated at the joining of the rivers Camowen and Drumragh to form the Strule. Like our rivers, Omagh people are quiet, peaceful, and unassuming. We have, through no fault of our own, inherited the title of the place of the worst atrocity of the Troubles.

On Saturday 15th August 1998 a Vauxhall Cavalier, which was stolen some time earlier, was driven into Omagh shortly before three o'clock in the afternoon. The car was parked close to a drapery shop selling back-to-school uniforms as the school holidays were drawing to an end. Two men primed the bomb and scurried out of the town in a waiting car. A short time later either deliberate or confusing warnings by the bombers resulted in the shoppers being pushed into the location of the bomb. The result being twenty-nine innocent men, women and children and two unborn twins were killed, and countless others physically and mentally scared. The deceased included tourists and visitors from Buncrana in Donegal and some as far away as Spain.

There has been much written about this atrocity and the public grieving people in Omagh, who had the added burden of trying to grieve in full view of the world's media. Amateur video photography of the event captured the horrific scenes showing men, women and children who were injured, dazed and confused as they covered the dead and treated the injured while others with only their bare hands sifted through the rubble for any possible survivors.

Those who perished on that fateful day were given no choice about what happened. There was a massive outpouring of emotion, anger and a quest for justice that as of this moment has never been addressed. Many to this day find it too painful to recount the events and almost 30 years on have had to carry the pain of suffering inflicted upon innocent people who were powerless to avoid this terrorist act. The Omagh victims had no choice about what took place that fateful day. Some families tried to deal with their loss by talking publicity while others declined to be interviewed or even talk about it. Many people had to deal with survivor's guilt, the 'why not me' syndrome as they witnessed their friends and neighbours living a nightmare while they could only look on feeling a total sense of helplessness. The entire community went into mourning that day regardless of whether they knew one of the victims or not. The PSNI informed me sometime later that Jonathan and I were behind the car carrying the bomb as it travelled into Omagh that day. This indiscriminate lottery could have easily included ourselves. We were just lucky.

The town itself was another victim; some argue it still hasn't recovered. This public outrage had the potential to cave in to the will of those who planted the bomb, those who wanted to bring about a bloody war and return to civil unrest. However the strong willed community condemned the massacre and made sure these victims would be the last.

This event is a prime example of community trauma. It really was a case that everyone knew someone affected by the bombing. We must have the courage to look for positive meaning in the most tragic experience. We can in time look at these events and how this experience can enrich our lives and the lives of others. I refer to the experience of the late Gordon Wilson from Enniskillen. He lost his beautiful daughter Marie in what is now referred to as the poppy day massacre at the War Memorial on Sunday 8th November 1987.

As he and his daughter lay in the rubble they exchanged their words of unconditional love for each other and his offer of forgiveness sent a message around the world that unconditional love can never be broken even in death.

His experience catapulted this self-effacing shopkeeper onto the world stage and his example of acceptance was, I believe, a pivotal moment when we began to realise that we must put down our swords and embrace a better way.

Losing a Baby, Miscarriage, Still born and Infant Loss:

The experience of losing a baby before full term or shortly afterwards is one of the most difficult bereavements anyone can face. Despite the fact that the child did not grace this earth for any length of time, its passing will take you on a grief journey that may result in you suffering post-traumatic stress disorder (PTSD) which is more often reserved and associated with violence and trauma, such is the depth of pain for these losses. Often these types of losses are not really recognised as grief because the child who has died did not enjoy being known except for a few people, and this traumatic event has the potential to cause serious relationship difficulties. Society will allow a few days of mourning and you are expected to return to work with very few people having any real idea of how you might be feeling. Sometimes mothers whose infants are stillborn or die soon after birth are not always encouraged to see or hold the baby.

The death of a child is an unexplainable pain causing intense feelings of loss that can't be measured by their short presence, but will leave a legacy of a lifetime of what could have been. A wife who loses a husband is called a widow, a husband who loses a wife is called a widower. A child who loses his parents is called an orphan. Sadly we have no word for a parent who loses a child.

The death of a baby throws so much into the unknown. Parents will wonder why their baby died and can experience anger and feel let down by the doctors and medical staff. You will forever wonder what the baby would have looked like and how their family would have been perfect and complete if the baby who brought such love, joy and potential, had lived. There can be even more added trauma if the parents are told that the baby has died but labour still has to be induced. Sorrow and silence give way to feelings that once held such promise of hope, joy and happiness. The silent tears of grieving parents as they leave the maternity hospital mixed with the audible sounds of crying newborn babies, floral bunting and family celebration is unimaginable. Instead of celebrations, arrangements must be made to collect a tiny casket from the morgue or funeral home.

Then the hardest question, should they give the baby a name? What type of funeral ritual and should we have photographs etc? Often parents are given advice in an effort to comfort them but that can add even more pain by saying things like, '*It wasn't meant to be*' or '*at least you now know you can have another baby.*' What if the death was part of a multiple pregnancy assisted by IVF and other babies have survived.

In an effort to try to ease the grief we concentrate on the surviving children which can make mourning more difficult for the parents. Well intentioned family and friends may try to influence their own religious and cultural response and inadvertently cause much pain and suffering. Often our inability to say anything speaks louder than some choreographed platitudes written on a sympathy card that can have the effect of making people feel worse. For the parents, they have to come to terms that their hello has unexpectedly become a goodbye.

Your Children:

'*Your children are not your children. They are the sons and daughters of life's longing for itself. They come through you but not from you, and though they are with you yet they belong not to you.*'

Wayne Dyer from 'You will see it when you believe it.

Chapter Nineteen
Endings and Conclusions.

In Memory of Our Not so Dearly Departed:

*'In your memory I will start another day without you in it.
In your memory I will laugh with everyone
who knew and loved your smile.
I will force myself to listen to your music
and sing through my tears.
In your memory I will take chances,
say what I feel and hold back no joy.*

*I will travel and love you from the highest sources.
I will share your smiles and honour your memory by rebuilding
my life in ways you would want us both to do.
Because in your memory you deserve nothing less.
I may not hear your voice but my heart will continue to have con-
versations with you every day.*

*When you left all the pictures came out
and on occasions I find another I forgot about.
Then I came to the realisation that there are no more pictures and
that's a very sad moment.
From now on you are frozen in a moment in a frame and I will
continue to change while you remain frozen
in the delusion of time.'*

Unknown

Grief Will Not Become my Home:

'I am scared that grief will become my home, so I force myself

to get out of bed, out of my pyjamas and out of my room. Grieving has become so familiar that I am scared that it has become part of my identity, woven into my skin for ever intertwined. So I force myself to smile, to take a walk outside of my house even if I tried to forget that grief has made me comfortably numb and I am scared that I won't even feel myself again. So I force myself to watch romantic movies and listen to music with lyrics that move me hoping my heart will recall feeling.'

(Shyran Marsh)

'If you feel tempted to hide your sorrow, please remember grief is not the price we pay for love, it's often the only thing we are left with, to show we loved at all.'

(Zoe Clark-Coates)

'I needed more time. The end came too fast. I needed more time. I needed more time to memorise every inch of your face and more time listening to the sound of your laugh. I needed more time to lay beside you whispering in the dark. I needed a thousand more tomorrow's and a thousand more I love yous. I needed more time.'

(Shyran Marsh, 'Leave Her Wild')

The Thought of Our Own Demise:

Possibly one of the most difficult parts of my training to become a bereavement support worker was when I was asked to consider my own passing away. As far as I am aware we human-beings are the only species that have the ability to contemplate our own passing. The old saying that we come into this world with nothing and we leave with nothing is difficult to comprehend. An unexpected passing may be your first encounter with bereavement and an awareness of our own mortality. We go to great lengths to avoid the reality of death, especially our own. I have found that if we can somehow face the fact that we shall pass away and deal with this certainty we can rebuild our meaning structure, to make the most of this gift of the life that we have in the now. It's very difficult to imagine a world without us and life going on in our absence. Maybe we should consider how it went on before we came here and maybe our egos won't contemplate the image of us never existing again, but when we face this inevitable fact it is actually very freeing.

In my counselling training we were asked to write our own obituaries which I found very challenging for me personally. It seemed a bit self-indulgent to write nice things about yourself and how others would interpret the message. On the positive side it can bring into focus that the gift of life is a special gift and should never be squandered by unnecessary negativity worrying about things we don't have control over.

The Gift or Burden of Inheritance:

I remember some years ago a wealthy business man passed away and in our conversation we wondered how much he would have left to his sons and my friend Tommy said immediately he left all of it. Sometimes we can find that due to a bereavement we have inheritance problems. You may be thinking how could this be a problem? From the outside, like my friend Tommy, we can see a wealthy person pass and assume their descendants will be fine for money.

The problems can arise if you married into this wealth and others from the outside think you have an abundance of worldly goods. The deceased's family may think they are more deserving of the inheritance than you and this can cause infighting and anguish. You may feel the money is more a curse than a blessing. Having this inheritance can, if not thought about properly, often add to increasing high levels of loneliness. We then have the added burden of how do I protect this and make it work efficiently. Even

176

changes that appear for the better can take a while to adjust to the new realisation that your life has changed in more ways than one. Sometimes a bereavement can cause complete devastation and on top of your grief you can find yourself homeless, or financially insecure, or having to give up your job to look after children or depended adults.

Never be afraid to ask for support and share your worries and concerns with people you trust and seek advice on how you might best manage your situation. Don't put unpaid bills away. If the person you have lost was the bread winner and took care of the financing side of the relationship you now have to learn to do things you may have never really considered. Seek advice from a well trusted, capable friend or financial adviser. In regards to debts ask for extended time and never think that you are going to be homeless or desuetude although this may seem like it is at the outset. We may have thought our lives were reasonably secure and now your whole world has been turned upside-down.

Bereavement has a way of making your whole world very insecure. It can be about making new friends and relationships which you question, are they sincere? What about your future, will there be enough to sustain me? You may have to decide to sell property and dispose of assets because it's impracticably to hold on to them. These assets may have been in the family for generations and here you find yourself having to make very difficult decisions. In our bereavement journey we have to examine our need for attachments.

'Our most Common Attachments:'
from *'You will see it when you believe it:'* by Wayne Dyer

Suffering can take many forms and is always played out in form. Our attachments to externals are unlimited. Overleaf he gives seven of our most common attachments.

1. *Attachment to Stuff* - Most of us in the Western world identify ourselves and our relative degree of success or failure by the quantity and quality of stuff we accumulate. We make such a connection that we attach our very worth as human beings to the acquisition of things. Consequently we can add to our suffering when we attach and identify ourselves by what we have accumulated, and by our need to be identified by who we are or what we own. When you adopt such a stance you set yourself up for perpetual frustration.

2. *Attachment to Other People* - This is one of the sickest attachments, and will create a great deal of suffering until we learn to overcome it in your life. I'm not saying it's inappropriate to love someone else, to value another person's presence in your life, and to celebrate your connect-ness. These are very positive results of creating unconditional love relationships in your life. I mean wanting or needing to own another and feeling useless, immobilized and hurt if that person is not part of your life in the way you desire. Such feelings are attachments. These are the relationships in which you give power and control over your own being to another, and they will always lead to suffering.

3. *Attachment to the Past* - Learning to be detached from the past and the traditions that are an important part of many people's lives is one way to eliminate some of the suffering that exists in our world. Take a look at all the people who are fighting in wars around the globe today and see the suffering and dying in the name of tradition. They are taught that what their ancestors believed they must believe. With logic they perpetuate the suffering in their own lives and in the lives of their assigned enemies. Many of these battles between ethnic groups have been waged for thousands of years. With this kind of attachment thinking that is taught within these cultures, the battles will last forever. The minds of those in such cultures are not

their own. They are living in form only dying for a tradition that guarantees enmity and hatred for generations to come

4. *Attachment to Your Form* - If you believe that you are only your body, and as it goes, so do you, then you are living in a lifetime of suffering. Wrinkles, hair loss, weakening vision and indications of physical change will create a sense of suffering in direct proportion to your attachment to remaining the same. This attachment to your body can create a lifestyle of artificiality and fear that will prevent from you being on your path and involved in your destiny. Attachment to your body as the means of fulfilment in this life results in an endless preoccupation with appearance. It is an attachment to the package that contains you, and it disguises the knowledge that your body is temporary form that you are occupying.

5. *Attachment to the Ideas of Being Right* - This is one of the most difficult attachments to discard. Being right could be considered a terminal Western disease. This attachment to being right creates suffering, because it is almost always a useless device for communicating with other people. If you cannot communicate effectively, you are going to suffer in your relationships. People do not want to be told how to think and that they are wrong if they disagree with you. When people encounter such a stance, they automatically shut you out of your consciousness, and a barrier has been erected. If you are being the one shut out it is because of your inability to listen. It is because you are so attached to what you already believe that you insist on making everyone who disagrees with you wrong. Attachments like these make loving relationships almost impossible to sustain, because boundaries are continuously being erected.

6. *Attachment to Money* - To be detached to the acquisition of money is a difficult undertaking. It is however, important if

you are to feel a strong sense of authentic choice making within your life. I have found that those who are able to do what they love and keep themselves focused on living that way have the amount of money they need come into their lives. They seem to keep the money circulating, using it to serve others rather than letting the accumulating of capital and cost of things be the dominate themes in life. They do not suffer from more disease that is so prevalent in our culture.

7. *Attachment to Winning* - Winning is almost an addiction in our culture, and as long as we are attached to the need to win we will experience some suffering as a result. Once again it is important to emphasize, I am not against winning. I love to win as much as anyone, particularity when I engage in athletic contests. We suffer when we do not emerge as the winner. A great test of character is how we react when we lose.

'Gifted by Grief'

Jane Duncan Rogers (Written with permission from the author)

This is an excellent memoir of her husband and a must read for anyone going through the grieving journey. I won't spoil it by saying too much but suffice to say it is about her unrelenting love and is a deeply moving account of a married couple's journey through terminal cancer. This may sound a sad and not a pleasant read but it is the exact opposite. It is a most inspirational book dedicated to her husband Philip who had, during his cancer journey, recorded a warm and practical memory of his illness. Her journey begins when his ends. The form of their relationship may have changed but if we really think about it, that is all that happens, we change from the physical to the non-physical. Our bodies may die but our essence or soul will keep each other company. Her memoir will take you on a journey helping the reader to forgive the past and heal our future leading us to a rebirth.

Anticipated Grief - Death is not a Punishment, it's a Transition:

'Some people are slowly taken, often losing one memory a day. As they are taken from us we stand and watch as they are pulled away from us, as doctors give both diagnoses and prognoses and offer little more than palliative support. Often our relationship can change when these types of diagnoses are presented. By virtue of our relationship we become the carer and the loved one becomes the cared for. Like many relationships this is not always an easy arrangement. The boundaries have now changed and no matter how much we love someone we can and will often experience compassion fatigue.

There may only be so much you can give until you find yourself completely exhausted and enraged as you try to juggle your family life and some sense of normality in the family unit. I have lost count of the times when a bereaved person confides in me that they had wished the person to die and are now racked with guilt for having such thoughts when the relief that the loved one is no longer in pain moves to a state of loneliness and regret. I would remind them that your anger is focused on the disease and not your loved one. Your wishing the person dead is just your wanting an end to the painful experience.

When a terminal prognosis is given often the relationship will change with a partner. The role can change to care giver and often there is only so much you can give as you suspend any normal activity and standing by helplessly as you witness your loved one slipping away one moment at a time. We may have to make decisions in relation to how this expected bereavement will end and what, if any, choices can we make to make the expected ending easier for everyone affected.'

(Jane Duncan Rogers)

Endings:

Often the question arises, should we discuss endings with our loved one?

Unfortunately no two situations are the same and no one size fits all. Some will want to discuss their passing and others will choose not to. The only thing to remember is that when you have this discussion you can never go back. The trend in modern medicine is, tell the patient the whole truth and give a time frame. Often we place our medical team in such high esteem we allow their best guess to become a countdown clock for their passing. If you are the next of kin then you should have a major say in regards how and what should be discussed.

Other family members will have different views and I would say only do what you do from a place of love and not what is deemed correct or what others might think.

Final Arrangements:

This is a time for clear heads and if your loved one is able and aware then you may want to have such a discussion. If not don't stress you will never get this wrong:

- Try to make sure any last wills and testaments are up to date to avoid serious misunderstanding later.
- Decide on a funeral director.
- Do they want a public or private wake, or funeral home?
- Cremation or burial?
- What they want done with the ashes etc?
- Who you would like to have present and deliver the eulogy?

In my own journey, Marian wouldn't discuss this with me. She only said, *'you will know what to do.'* She did say however she had been keeping nice underwear in her wardrobe for a special occasion and to use them. That one statement taught me never to keep things for the right time. The right time is now when we can appreciate it before the choice is taken away from us.

After Death:

This is when it gets real because now your loved one is removed from the conversation and cannot make decisions. From now on you can only guess what they would have liked and no amount of preparation will ever be enough. Reach out to close family and friends to support you if possible.

Make a list of what needs to be done and who to contact. Find a good reputable funeral director and be advised by them on the procedure, they are well used to these situations and very professional. They will be able to advise you on how to proceed. They will advise you on the various costs associated with the funeral and, on your instruction, will be able to make any necessary arrangement fitting your budget and what would be expected. This will save a lot of unnecessary stress.

God and the Afterlife - What should you Believe?

Religion should only exist to bring joy and clarity. In bereavement support, clients will often be reluctant to discuss their belief or lack of just in case of causing offence or assume I would not share their ideology. Others may fear that I might have an agenda to promote my own particular brand of religion or atheism. If I was to say I believe in God then it begs the question, do I share your interpretation of God and the rules associated with that religion? Unfortunately in this part of the world we have the added burden of culture into the mix. Faith can bring comfort and joy and anyone is entitled to find their salvation in any religion they choose.

My observation at one time led me to believe that Church and State in Ireland had a vested interest in keeping people apart. These two great powers would have at one time had sought to coerce their subjects into holding beliefs that benefit people in power. According to Dr Dorothy Rowe beliefs are ideas. Ideas are things we create, and as we create them, we can change them. There is no set of religious or philosophical beliefs which ensures that we are always secure and happy. Like everything in life, whatever the belief it has advantages and disadvantages. However, according to Dr Rowe, it is possible to create a set of beliefs expressed in our own individual way, using the metaphors which are rich in meaning for us, with which we can draw strength and optimism.

Whether we like it or not religion in the 21st century still dominates our lives. Our faith can give us great courage and comfort in times of loss or when danger threatens us. Religion in Ireland today is a bit like a child's comfort blanket. When the child gets confused it looks for its blanket for reassurance. In Ireland many different Christian Churches are pretty much influenced by what I would call the just world indoctrination. That simply put allows the followers of any faith to make the rules in regard to how we conduct our lives. If we simply obey the rules, fine, but if we dare to question we are seen as the enemy and often treated like so. I see little or no difference in what the Christian Churches do or say.

Some would argue that Church rules should be similar to the rules of say a golf club and if the members don't agree then they can find another club that fits their value structure and proclaim their invisible friend is more important than someone else's. Church attendance has been desecrated especially since the outbreak of COVID when we were not allowed public worship. Many believers now choose to sit in the comfort of their own homes and watch the service on the webcam without the need to participate in the service.

Community Support During Bereavement:

In Ireland we had, and in some cases still have, the blueprint on grief. Every community has smaller communities called family. On learning the news of someone's passing the community members instinctively know what to do. They will organise and surround the bereaved to allow them time to grieve. In Ireland during the wake we don't speak of the deceased in the past terms. The body is kept in the house for approximately three days and you will hear countless people who visit say, *'sorry for your trouble.'*

The bereaved family are not expected to do anything other than meet and greet visitors allowing themselves to constantly repeat the story of how they passed. At the time the bereaved will be expected to repeat the story continuously but in fact what is happening is the bereaved are also talking to themselves and slowly the realisation that they have lost someone very close to them sinks in allowing them time to realise the enormity of the situation. During this time the family will see and talk to countless neighbours and friends who will recall happier times spent in the company of their bereaved.

Sometimes apologies are offered for any disputes or misunderstandings and new friendships can be made into new generations. Unfortunately in recent times, and exasperated by Covid, the whole scaffolding for bereavement that would have been erected is now redundant. While me may like and expect privacy we may need help to absorb the shock of bereavement. If you find yourself in a state of shock and unable to process the enormity of the loss please see this as nothing more than a sedative to help stop you from falling apart.

Often people can't imagine how the rest of the world is going on as normal when you are facing what you might think is total annihilation. We may feel a sense of guilt about what we should have said or done. Relationships can come crashing down, but on a positive note new relationships can be built. Guilt can also be a positive when you accept you can't go back, but you can learn to be a better person in the hope of a more fruitful future. We are rightly taught never to speak ill of the dead but also don't make a saint of the person who has died. Sometimes the dead need forgiveness too. Sometimes we may exclude children in an effort to protect them but children are very perceptive and will pick up signals. Your tone about the bereavement is more important than the substance and allow children to cry as it will give them ownership of their loss in time to come.

Putting time into your grieving is important. Couples who experience the loss of a child will find themselves on different journeys. People often say a child's bereavement can bring a couple together. In fact the opposite is true. Blame and frustration and being unable to express their grief can be extremely difficult for a couple to deal with. It requires a great deal of time and support from family and friends. When engaging with couples, in cases of pregnancy loss or miscarriage always take your lead from the couple. Some well-meaning family and friends will talk nonstop to avoid any awkward silences. Some couples may not want to discuss or share their painful episode, please honour this request. Ask for permission to help in any practical ways remembering always that this couples plans and dreams have been shattered. Avoid statements like you can try again or at least you didn't go full term. These well-meaning statements are very painful for parents to hear.
This is very often said when parents experience losing a child in a cot death and then often the blame game begins, *'why didn't you check on the child?'*

Sometimes in bereavement we can suffer from what I would call phantom pains. By that I mean we can go into a shop to buy something for a loved one knowing that they will never wear or use that item. Muscle memory when you automatically pick up a favourite drink or item for the deceased only to get home and realise they are not there to receive it. We can swear we can see them in a crowded street and run to find them only to be disappointed that under closer inspection they look nothing like your loved one. These abnormal thoughts are absolutely normal but can be very painful and we are often ashamed to mention our feelings for fear of being regarded and losing control of our mind.

There is More to Life than Grief:

One of the things I found most difficult was the disbelief that Marian had gone away. At the beginning it seemed impossible that my world could continue when I no longer had my wife and our children had no mother. While I could understand that she had been ill for a long time, the reality of her passing was, at the beginning, too difficult to contemplate.

A part of me was in denial and I was holding on to a portion of disbelief. The unfairness of life soon gave way to silent rage. I can very well remember just before Christmas trying to choose presents and buying food for the Christmas dinner while screaming inside as the jolly festive music rang out in our local shopping centre. That first Christmas I remember just abandoning the shopping trolley in the middle of the isle and getting into my car and headed off to another town almost 30 miles away to try to complete my shopping. I knew I wouldn't have to meet family or friends and I could break down without attracting stares from people who might see me fall apart.

That Christmas I would agonise over trying to buy something that I knew Marian would have liked, her favourite foods were picked up but left on the shelf again. Marian loved the whole Christmas experience. While I didn't buy into all the hype I was happy to allow her to experience this and indulged in the ritual of buying presents etc.

After she passed I felt the need to try to make Christmas as normal as possible. I didn't know it then but I was suffering what is known as phantom pain for the dead which I touched upon above. We have often heard of people who lose a limb but can still feel pain in a foot that is no longer there. This can and does happen in grief as well. We can purchase items for our loved ones knowing they will never enjoy them.

It took me a long time to lock the back door in case I was asleep in the middle of the night and she would be unable to get into the house. When I look back I think I was switching between two realities. My brain was allowing me to function on one level and at the same time I was in a state of denial. I, like many others, was coping on the outside with normal day-to-day situations and at the same time trying to wrestle with heart-wrenching painful problems, trying to make sense of the death experience. I seemed to have accidentally become a lifelong member of a club with no benefits or recognition, except a big empty hole in my world.

I learned that grief can be a heavy load to carry. I could also see others in this club too and while I tried to see their grief I learned that all grief is different and never the same.

Shortly after her passing the sympathy messages and ready-to-eat dinners stopped coming and family and friends soon went back to their own lives. Elisabeth Kubler-Ross and her stages of grief were not to be seen in my world as I struggled to find structure in my life while denial, anger, bargaining and depression were all playing musical chairs in my head. My denial was hoping that she would walk in the back door again any minute while at the same time I was trying to process the fact that she was never coming home again. Much later on I realised that my delusional mind was playing tricks on me but the reality was that my mind was affording me moments away from the feelings of despair and pain. This process, while difficult to make sense of at the time, was a vital component and helpful coping strategy with a long-term aim to re-live my pain and take me to a path of learning on how to cope with the new normal which was now my life. This form of delusional behaviour has made survival possible.

When I Die:

'When my coffin is being taken out
You must never think I am missing this world.
Don't shed any tears.Don't lament or feel sorry.
I am not falling into a monster's abyss.

When you see my corpse is being carried
Don't cry for my leaving.
I am arriving at eternal love.
When you leave me in the grave don't say goodbye.
Remember a grave is only a curtain for the paradise behind.

You'll only see me descending into a grave, now watch me rise.
How can there be an end when the sun sets,
or the moon goes down.
It looks like the end. It seems like a sunset, but it is a dawn.
When the grave locks you up that is when your soul is freed.

Have you ever seen a seed fallen to the earth
not rise with a new life.
Why should you not rise with a new life. Why should you doubt
the rise of a seed named human.

Have you ever seen a bucket lowered into a well coming back
empty, when it can come back like Joseph from the well.
When for the last time you close your mouth your words and soul
will belong to the world of no place no time.'

Rumi

Chapter Twenty
Letting Go.

How do you rebuild after a loss? Is it possible to rewrite history and start again? You may have shared too many dreams, laughter and fun times, your heart and head are saying different things. We know we can't turn back time. Can we be happy with our loved one only existing in our memories?

There is hope for a new tomorrow! There will come a time when you have carried your grief for long enough. Only you get to decide. Putting down your grief takes great courage because in our minds we can confuse rebuilding as a way of shutting out our memories. Letting go does not mean erasing the past, it simply means that you're open to the possibility of making new memories.

There will come a time when holding on is too much and no matter how good it once was, memories won't sustain you. Change is never easy.

We can fight to hold on or we can fight to let go. We can throw down our sword and embrace our grief enemy. Choose not to be sad for what has ended. Just be glad they were once yours.
The bad news is you will never really get over the loss. The good news is they will live forever in your struggle, shouting support from the sideline of your heart. When our hearts understand this it can let go and you can grow.

The more you risk the more vulnerable you become, one of life's ironies.

190

Finding an Inner Light - A Mother's Reflection:

Bereavement and times of crisis shake up our stable world and we can be left with the feeling that nothing will ever be the same again. We are forced to make adjustments in how, where and when we work, in how we spend our leisure time and how we relate to family and friends.

Inner healing begins when we stop clinging to a better yesterday and take the first step towards making a better tomorrow. If we are to survive a crisis and beyond it, to again find hope and the joy of life, we can find a way by thinking new thoughts and believing new things about our lives.

It can be painful to face the facts of our experience and the crisis it has created, yet this is the first step to becoming whole again. At such times when we reach deep within ourselves we will find hidden strength, courage and hope, which we never knew existed. And when we feel we could not possibly be strong or have courage or find hope, these resources are there within us, waiting to be found.

When we look around us we find that others too have known such things to be true. In times past another who understood this, recognised the possibility that those who mourn could exchange beauty for ashes, again find joy instead of sorrow and feel praise instead of despair.

An extract from the writings of John O'Donohue from his book *'Eternal Echoes'*

'It's utterly astonishing how the force and fibre of each day unravel into the vacant air of yesterday. You look behind you and you see nothing of your days here. Our vanished days increase our experience of absence, yet our past does not deconstruct as

191

it never was. Memories is the place where our vanished days secretly gather. Memory rescues experience from total disappearance. The kingdom of memory is full of the ruins of presence. It is astonishing how faithful experience actually is, how it never vanishes completely. Experience leaves deep traces in us. It is surprising that years after something has happened to you, the needle of thought can hit some groove in the mind and music of a long vanished event can rise in your soul as fresh and vital as the evening it happened.'

The Healing Game, Getting out of Limp Mode:

Our consciousness is our greatest gift. We give great attention to the energy outside ourselves and often chose to ignore the energy within. Learning to create new thoughts and holding on to thoughts of healing which generate emotion requires much expenditure of energy. During our mourning period this energy may be in very short supply.

Have you ever noticed that when we are absolutely unable to face any type of normality in our day that food, alcohol or any other type of stimulant will not ease our pain. We shut down to survive, cutting out any offers of help from anyone in order to cope. We don't even allow ourselves to consider any encouragement or opportunities of support or advice from friends, family or professionals.

If you are familiar with modern cars you will sometimes experience what is called limp mode. This a system that is designed to protect the engine of your car by greatly reducing the power to the engine while still allowing just enough power to get you home. This is not dissimilar to how you can feel when trying to cope after a bereavement. You can just about get one foot past the other and while you manage the essentials of life, but in reality you are far from fully engaging. Unlike cars we don't have the recourse

192

of a mechanic to fall back on and instead will have to carefully examine our thinking and question our low mood. Failure to do this will result in your life shutting down in order to protect you from your pain.

If you can cast your mind back to when you were a teenager and your first love. The person you thought you loved leaves you suddenly and without warning taking with them all your dreams, joy, laughter and sense of self. You may have found yourself spending days or weeks in bed not eating or being able to work. You may have lost the drive to engage in your normal activities and life for you was not worth living any-more. Then out of nowhere you get a call from this person saying that they are very sorry for their actions and want to meet you and make things right again. Out of nowhere you find this burst on energy, jump into the shower, tidy up your room and embrace life once again. Where does this energy come from? Not from the food you haven't eaten or the sleepless nights when you paced your bedroom floor. It comes from a place deep inside, an inner knowing that we find difficult to explain to ourselves and others. Bereavement robs you of any such phone call despite our longings and dreams. It's robs us of our hope.

If you imagine that loss is like an indescribable pain in your heart and that this pain can sometimes be unbearable, then in order for you to ease the pain you learn not to talk about it or discuss your feelings. You instead invent clever ways not to show anyone your wounded broken heart. Imagine your heart has a huge wooden splinter buried deep inside it and impossible to dislodge. The only way to avoid suffering this pain inflicted by your loss is by creating a shielded life that never gets exposed to or experiences joy ever again.

You avoid ever being open to any possibility of healing and instead you build a wall to protect the possibility that exposure may cause you more excruciating pain. You now have the added burden of a painful heart and heavy protection wall to carry with you constantly. You put up these walls of protection to avoid the possibility of adding to the pain of loss you have experienced. We may think that behind these walls our heart is protected but it is now in a place of darkness. It carries a heavy burden and is sealed tight, leaving it impossible to ever find a way back to the person you once were. You are protecting your wounded heart so that it is never to be exposed to pain again. The end result is a heart that is so shut off that it strips you of any light and healing opportunities. No one is allowed access to your sacred place and the fear of suffering more pain is unimaginable. Opening up our heart from this place is an extremely difficult task but it can be done. You build these walls and you can take them down again. This is the time to summon up the courage to relieve the pain and instead of closing down to protect ourselves we face our pain in a new way with an open heart, to a journey to happiness that is your birthright and we must take the opportunities to start to live again.

Working out your own healing will take great courage and will from the outset seem counter-intuitive. We must learn to listen to our intuition from what I would call our internal silent partner or internal monologue. The silent partner is the continuous voice that is always talking to us and has an opinion about how we manage our lives. Did you ever sit down to watch a film or read a book and if you were sufficiently interested then you would give the activity your full undivided attention. But what happens when you begin to lose interest? This is when your silent partner begins to speak to you on any topic that has crossed your mind earlier. This voice can jump in and criticise you and play havoc with your life. What is this voice and why does it come and go into your head at will.

We find it very difficult and sometimes impossible to keep control of our thoughts. These voices/feelings come and go at will uninvited. The ultimate trick is to stay open to these voices while at the same time filter out any negative self-talk or allow it to dictate how you think. From now on you will refuse to be willing to close your heart down and instead you will face the pain. You will instead allow the pain to have its way but from now on only on your terms leaving the real you to honour and respect your feelings of loss. I encourage you to learn to stay open and embrace the raw pain, and slowly over time learn to remove the protection that was closing down your beautiful spirit. Let the light in and shine through your brokenness. Your darkness in your heart is the absence of light.

We have the power to exercise control over our pain, but the fear of the pain encourages us to protect ourselves. However overprotection inhibits our ability to heal from our grief. The price of healing is not closing your heart off to pain and suffering. Closing your heart is a habit and like all habits can be broken with repetition. You may have a natural reaction to put your walls up when someone triggers you but you must resist the urge. We must learn to do the opposite of our initial desire.

What I call our silent partner or what others would describe as ego, has been with us since childhood and will stay until we leave this world. From now on you must challenge this internal monologue and remember it's your fear that is trying to protect you. The real you not is not the voice of doubt and criticism that is always quick to judge you. You don't have to fight this voice or battle with the extreme thoughts, but keep asking yourself is my internal voice really correct and is what I am thinking really true? Can my new thinking guide me to a better conclusion. Your self-talk will continue but when you apply your new energy through repetition then in time this chatter will give way to your new thought patterns. Just remember your aim is not to continue the trauma, pain and anxiety you have experienced. You are healing to allow joy and happiness back into your life again. When you can learn how to elevate stress you will sense your new connection and enthusiasm for life. We need to learn the art of emotional regeneration and need to find our power and zest for life because if we don't then the traumatic events in our life will have gained control over our thoughts. From now on we need to decide to stop needing to be rescued. We may have only one life but we get countless opportunities to find different versions of ourselves.

Fear of our Own Death:

The fear of our own death is awakened sharply when we are facing grief and loss. I have come to know after many years that our own fear of death is often the opposite of what we may think. Death certainly takes from us, but it is also a giver, a giver of meaning.

A few years ago, I had to come to terms with what began as a minor illness turning into a cancer journey. I could see it was both a taker and a giver. The long months in a Belfast hospital forced me to totally revaluate my thinking as I had to contemplate the end of my existence. However it also brought me the freedom to explore the meaning of my life. No one wants to ever struggle with the idea of their own mortality. I don't suggest we dwell on this every hour of every day. I'm suggesting that sometimes we might just pause for a moment just to ponder the idea. My health journey has taught me to accept each day/week as a wonderful gift. I have learned that trying to avoid or being reluctant to contemplate such an event will lead to a life of stress and worrying that can actually lead to illness.

We can try to avoid thinking about our own death and imagine it as some sort of accident that we have no control over because we have been conditioned not to get close to death. We can't see the bigger picture that we have much less to fear or face than we have thought. Our awareness of death and the nature of death was the preserve of our clergy. Only now, in the hospice or palliative care system, can we get the opportunity to talk and contemplate our own demise. Learning to live and learning to die are different sides of the same coin. The realisation of our mortality encourages us to make full use of our time here on earth. The earlier we do this, the sooner we can lead a life of psychological, as in spiritual growth. This will allow us to find great joy in what we would have previously considered the mundane. We can find contentment in the most simplest and basic pursuits.

Oasis in the Desert – My Journey Through Grief:

When I look back at my story, I can only describe it as a journey through a vast desert. While I was aware of the pain of loss and unrelenting heat of grief, I lumbered day to day on my grief journey. As I stumbled forward, I found the odd patch of green oasis and some living water in the form of friends who would sit with my pain and didn't judge. They didn't offer to do anything other than allow me to feel my pain, reassuring me that I was not totally alone.

I was blessed with good family and friends. The passing years have shown me that my tragic loss was also an opportunity for me to grow spiritually and when I could allow myself to grow, some amazing things began to happen in my life. When I finally accepted the reality that I couldn't change the past, new ideas on how to rebuild my life would emerge. For me it was finding the courage to meet my grief and work with it, instead of resisting and denying the hopeless. I began to experience spiritual growth which taught me what I needed to know. I read that salutation and healing is the same word from the salve or the process of becoming whole again. A large part of my growing and evolving was learning to forgive and no longer blaming others for my pain.

I have tried to cover as best I can, the countless ways we can grieve our loss and this book was written for people to dip in and out of as and when they were able to. Together we have shared our journey and each of us has our own unique way of dealing with loss. It's been my experience that we never get it wrong, only different pathways to hopefully the same destination. You don't need anyone telling you how you should feel and don't be afraid to put time into your bereavement, as much time as you require. Our loved ones are too important in life to be forgotten in death.

Whether your loss experienece was sudden or expected, it can take great courage to ask for help or seek support, reaching out to a stranger. No one knows enough about this subject to be certain because we all grieve differently. Some people, myself included, would find it difficult to talk about how we feel and others have little or no such problems. The journey is a lonely one because when we are alone we must face our true selves. When the masks are all removed we have to face our pain alone. I was most fortunate knowing Marian would want me to rebuild my life so I could be happy again and I would have wanted the same for her. Not everyone is as lucky and can really struggle to come to terms with loss.

To my dear reader, thank you for journeying along these pages with me and we all have our own reasons for doing what we do. All our decisions in life will have consequences, some we may have predicated with great accuracy and others have fallout we could never have imagined.

My abiding wish for you is that your memory and your imagination will be free from the pain of bereavement. I leave you with the beautiful memory of my late mother-in-law who had end stage Alzheimer's. Upon seeing our children come into her room she said, *'I may not know your name but I know I love you.'* I celebrate the place in you where we are all one.

Dedications

I dedicate this book in memory of Marian McGurgan 1954-2000, who loved her family by allowing the father to do the providing, the mother the deciding and the children the overriding.

To our children Jonathan, Maria and daughter-in-law Mellissa, without whose constant support this book would have remained a collection of words on my computer. (Johnny could have done the editing a bit quicker though).

To my friend John McCusker for his dedication in helping me turn my thoughts into words and allowing me to just write what I feel and he would do the rest.

To my late parents John and Sadie and sister Rosemary; to my brothers and sisters - some people are born lucky and others come from large families.

To Owen McCrystal (Godfather).

To all the McDermott Family.

To my countless friends and clients who will remain nameless, who had the courage to trust me with their grief story. It was an honour to share your experience. I wish I had your courage.

To Evelyn McAleer and her husband Jim Kerr for your encouragement and prodding me to finally get it to the printers. Thanks for your wonderful friendship. Without your support this book would never have got out of my head onto paper.

To Roley and Mervyn from Cruse Bereavement Support who both know more about bereavement support than I will ever know. Thank you for all your mentoring and support.

Father Brian D'Arcy.

Declan Forde (Partner in Crime).

Frank Galligan.

Declan Coyle.

In memory of Dr Dorothy Rowe 1930-2019 who I was privileged to call a friend, confidant and mentor who gave me the courage to train in bereavement support.

Billy & Elizabeth Nixon.

Peter (the Ghost) Campbell.

Jullian Elliot.

Tommy Campbell.

Gerry & Mary McGread.

My thanks to the following for assisting me in so many ways and to those whose names do not appear but you know who you are:

Julia & Sharon for proof reading early drafts.

Hazel Short, Care for Cancer.

Clare Adair for the banter and encouragement.

Our friends in the Omagh Committee of Cancer Research UK.

Richard McElrea.

Terry McDonnell.

Toni & Brian McFarline.

Joe Cuthbertson.

John Slane.

This book would not have been possible without the support I received from the Mastery Foundation (The Ireland Initiative) for peace and reconciliation and my cousin Mary McCartan who encouraged me to take a few days to share my thoughts and feelings in the safe environment of Dromantine Monastery Conference Centre. They gave me the inspiration to write about my bereavement experience.

Testimonial

Over many years of working with clients I have received many thank you cards and I only include this one to encourage you to reach out and take risks in supporting someone going through a bereavement. Sometimes we don't know the impact our presence can have:

'A million thanks will not be enough to express my gratitude to you. Thank you for helping me survive the most difficult time I ever had to face in my life. Your valuable advice, supportiveness, non-judgemental guidance, kindness and compassion held me together when I felt I had no one to talk to.

You listened, encouraged me and believed in me to keep going and make healthy decisions when days and nights were very dark. I would not be here today writing this card if it was not for you as I had no one to turn to. I feel so lucky that our paths have crossed.'

Anonymous

Recommended Further Reading

The following is a list of books & Authors who inspired and helped me both in my own grief journey as well as when I was writing this book. I would highly recommend any of their work to aid you in your own journey.

- *'Ask and it is Given'*
  Abraham Hicks

- *'I can see Clearly Now'*
  Dr Wayne Dyer

- *'Wanting Everything'*
  Dr Dorothy Rowe

- *'Mans Search for Meaning'*
  Victor Frankl

- *'The Power Of Now'*
  Eckhart Tolle

- *'The Road Less Travelled'*
  M. Scott Peck

- *'12 Rules for Life'*
  Jordan Peterson

- *'The Untethered Soul'*
  Michael A. Singer

Notes.

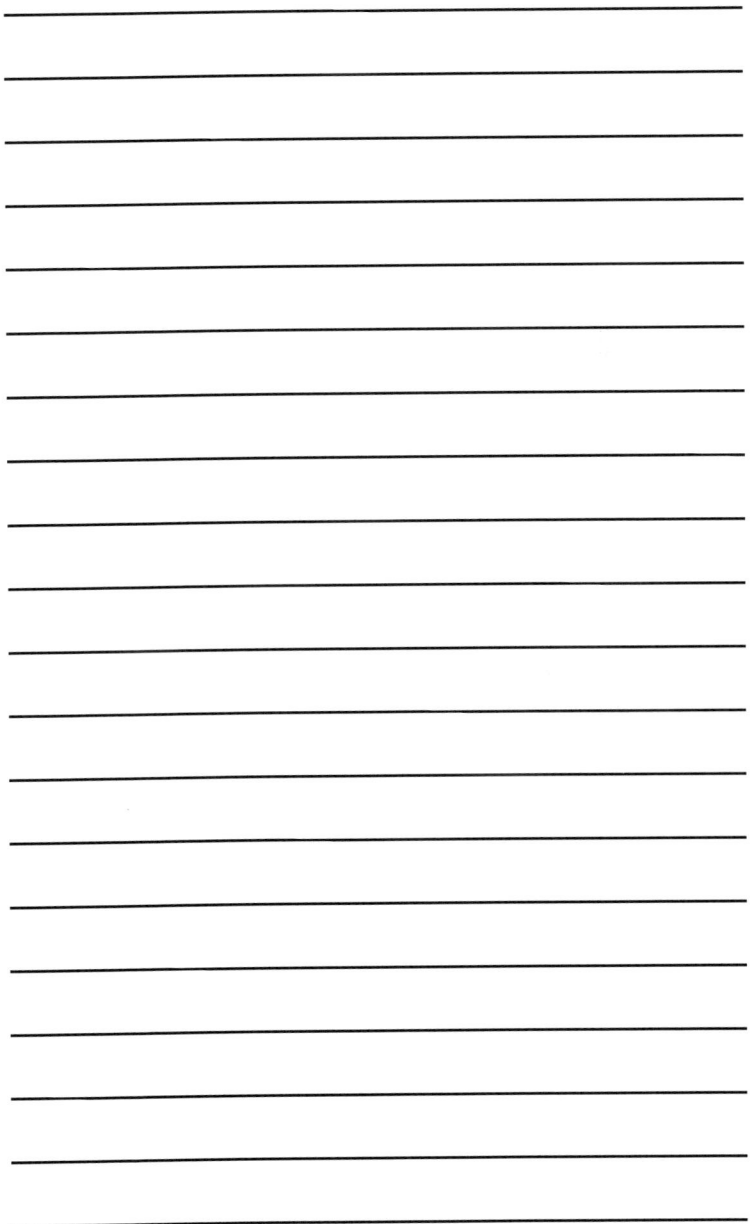